PRE'
Broken
DOLLS

Who Will be King?

KER DUKEY & K WEBSTER

Pretty Broken Dolls
Copyright © 2017 Ker Dukey and K. Webster

ISBN-13: 978-1977566041
ISBN-10: 1977566049

Cover Design: All By Design
Photo: Adobe Stock
Editor: Word Nerd Editing - www.wordnerdediting.com
Formatting: Champagne Book Design

ALL RIGHTS RESERVED. This book contains material protected under International and Federal Copyright Laws and Treaties. Any unauthorized reprint or use of this material is prohibited. No part of this book may be reproduced or transmitted in any form or by any means, electronic or mechanical, including photocopying, recording, or by an information and retrieval system without express written permission from the Author/Publisher.

This is a work of fiction. Names, characters, places, and incidents either are the product of the author's imagination or are used fictitiously, and any resemblance to actual persons, living or dead, business establishments, events, or locales is entirely coincidental.

Betrayal and rage, a festering sting.
Monster vs Master. Who will be king?

Damaged and desperate, a solution they must find,
To bring back the dolly who is one of a kind.

Disloyalty and failure will not be forgiven.
Seeking revenge, the monster is driven.

Hungry for his affection, our master has waited.
These broken dollies lives have already been fated.

The storm is upon us, the chaos raining down,
Now that the big players have come to town.

Who will come out breathing with their prize by their side?
And who will be collateral damage along for the ride?

DEADICATION

To our pretty little dolls,

Thank you for always coming back for more.
You take the pain and the abuse and the torment.
And we enjoy doling it out.

Yours,
Monster and Master
aka
K&K

"There are no heroes.
In life, the monsters win."

~ *Sansa* ~

A Game of Thrones by George R.R. Martin

CHAPTER ONE

~ *Damaged* ~

Viktor aka Tanner
Russia – Age Eighteen

Flames flicker from the fireplace heating the room to an unbearable degree. I told Veronika, our maid, not to light the fire tonight, but she did it anyway. She's getting too old to do her job, but she's been here longer than I have, so Father won't replace her. It's futile to even ask.

Sweat beads and drips down my back, the room expanding like it's alive with its own pulse. Nervous energy crackles and pops in my veins. The month is upon us—the time I get to prove myself to our father.

All Vasiliev men take part in The V Games when they come of age, to prove their worth and position within the family.

Our name and reputation means everything to our father.

Yuri Vasiliev.

His empire in the criminal world is matched by none.

Trafficking of women, guns, and drugs are all a front—a mask that truly hides what our family does. We delve into the darker depravities of all men *and* women, and once he gets you wound up in his world, where he's able to pull your strings and you'll follow, he never lets go.

He feeds your urges. You'll worship him for it. A true puppet master. And I fucking idolize him with every ounce of my being. I want to be just like him, but most of all, I want to gain his respect.

With his plans to branch out his operation to the United States, I want to be the one he turns to and head the expansion. Wherever Father casts his net, I shall pull in his catch. Because that's what our family does. We own the world—even if they don't know it yet.

Soft footfalls creep across the hardwood floors, but the size of the silhouette looming over the room like a phantom doesn't match the dainty steps.

"Vlad, how do you cause such little sound with your movements?" I ask, swiveling my head to see my older brother almost gliding into the room. A motherfucking shadow. Stalking. Lurking. Waiting. Always shrouded in darkness.

The corners of his mouth curl into a devious smile and his amber eyes that match mine narrow as he studies me intently. Coming to a halt in front of me, he crosses his arms over his chest, the muscles beneath straining against the fabric of his suit.

"It's a skill all men like us should master, brother," he states in a matter of fact tone, a smirk on his dark, stubbly face. Vlad is a spitting image of our father. Tall, well over six and a half feet, and broad shouldered. His nearly black hair is tousled on top, always styled in a way that's meant to look messy—almost as though he enjoys the small rebellion against Father. Father, with his hair clipped short on the sides to reveal the grey beginning to grow there, wears his same-colored hair slicked back and perfect.

My brother drops his attention to the arsenal I have prepared—an array of weapons ready for use. Picking up a blade from the kit I've laid out on the bed, he runs it across his palm, and a crimson slit swells in its wake.

"This is a good knife. You should use this one," he tells me, pulling a small piece of cloth from his pocket and cleaning the blade before wrapping it around his hand to stop the bleeding. "Are you ready for this, Viktor?" There's not concern in his tone, merely doubt, and that causes anger to build inside my chest.

"You've been preparing me for this my entire life," I grind out in response, my jaw tightening. "*You* played in The V Games. It's a rite of passage."

A vein pops in his neck and his eyes flare for a moment before his features soften. He reaches for me, his palm wrapping around the back of my skull, and brings me forward. My forehead comes to rest on his flexed, muscular shoulder. He's still at least six inches taller than me, despite my growth over the summer.

I'm a man now. Yet he's older. Wiser. *And fucking taller.* I'm not small by any means, but he always uses my height to mock me when I get under his skin. It's a weak, predictable move—one I see coming every time.

He gives me a heavy pat on my shoulder blade then he pushes me back, signaling his moment of brotherly affection is over. My brother is a hard man. Raised with an iron fist, just like me. And at only twenty-two, he's being groomed to take over our father's empire—the family dynasty.

"The first players have arrived," he says, another smirk playing on his lips. "There's one in particular I think you'll like." He clenches his fist and punches me playfully in the chest.

I crack my knuckles in anticipation.

I've known about The V Games since I was twelve years old. By fourteen, I was allowed to attend the screenings that aired via a channel buried deep in the dark web.

At sixteen, I attended the actual event as a spectator. Most boys my age went to soccer matches, and although the arena was just as big—just as impressive with the audience able to attend, bet, watch, root for their players—they were nothing alike.

Two totally different sets of rules. In The V Games—*our games*—it's a competition of brutality and pleasure, feeding the compulsions of the darkest minds.

The rich and privileged pay to watch.

The depraved and sadistic pay to play.

The poor play in hopes they come out victorious, and sell what they catch.

The rules are simple.

Hunt or be hunted.

Kill. Fuck. Or keep the prizes you catch.

Above all else: survive.

If you make it through to the end alive, the sky is the limit in terms of your bounty. If you've ever had a desire frowned upon by society, The V Games are a place to live it out.

Preparation for The V Games goes on for months and months. Each player is scrutinized, fully background checked, then valued by the elite members, including Father. These events are as underground as it gets. And they must be handled with the utmost secrecy. The players, attendees, and bidders are from all walks of life, but the post powerful identities need to remain anonymous.

Growing up, I learned the most powerful people are always the most corrupt, depraved souls roaming the earth. Their need for control is deep-rooted and often requires a darker outlet.

My father offers them this outlet in abundance, and because of the high profile clients he caters to, he is untouchable by the law, feared by other criminal entities, and most importantly, worshiped by his clientele.

"Come, Viktor," Vlad orders. "Eat with us."

I leave the weapons out on the bed, hoping Veronika slips while clearing them away and accidently takes her own eye out. Then, maybe, Father would have no choice but to allow her to retire.

"A woman is still useful with only one eye, brother," Vlad says in amusement, and it's then I realize I spoke my thoughts aloud. I must work on my loose tongue and schooling my features so I'm not so easily readable. Vlad always says a poker face can save a man's life and instill fear in even the bravest of souls.

"It's unsettling not being able to read another person's expression, Viktor, and having that edge could mean the difference between life and death."

"Where are the stock?" I ask, ignoring his jab about the maid. I'm eager to see who's been offered up like meat packets for others to abuse and toy with. Although I'm young, I still like to play with them.

"Being prepared. You will have your introduction profile created tomorrow. Later, I'll take you to see one of the girls. She will be fun to hunt and fuck." His lips curl back in a brief grin before he stalls his features and the stoic haze returns to his face.

Each player is put before an anonymous panel to determine their worth, then all players' profiles are available to the spectators. Requests can be made, and a spectator will offer a player money to perform acts for them to watch. This brings stone cold killers to The V Games just for the paycheck and makes people like me and other well-respected family members who are put forward vulnerable to assassination by disgruntled enemies.

Deaths that occur within the arena for The V Games can not be avenged after, it's all part of the game. Which makes entering all that more dangerous and admirable with people in the criminal world we live in.

Vlad's cell phone chimes from his pocket, and he holds his hand up, signaling he needs a minute. He stalks off in the opposite direction to the kitchen, so I make my way there, curious to see who he referred to when he said join *us* for dinner.

The house is unusually quiet compared to how commonly busy it is in the months leading up to The V Games. Father will be preoccupied with the preparations, therefore other business will not be the priority.

I prefer the house like this. Less coming and going. Peaceful.

Pushing through the doors, I stroll into the kitchen. The room usually has appliances and other cooking utensils, but it's currently empty and there is nothing laid out to eat. This must mean Vlad wants to go out to dinner.

My stomach growls in protest at the idea of waiting. I've been sweating out half my body weight in my bedroom with the fire on. I need something to keep me going. Usually when my brother gets a call and needs a minute, the minute turns into thirty. The fridge beckons me, and I find some cold meats inside. Just as I'm closing the door, a body collides into me, knocking the food to the floor as I hurtle into the counter.

Niko's body presses against mine, pinning me against the cabinets. "I thought that was you creeping in here," he growls against my ear.

I wasn't creeping, asshole.

His cock pushes against my ass, and I shove him away from me, spinning to face him. He's grinning, his chest rising and falling in excitement.

"So, you're who's joining us for dinner?" I sneer, and he advances on me. Rearing back my arm, I launch it forward and hit him with a closed fist to the face. His head snaps to the side, then he slowly brings his gaze back to me. Blood blooms on his bottom lip, the pad of his thumb smearing it before sucking it into his mouth. He smirks. "I've missed you."

"Fuck you," I reply, my tone cold like my heart.

"Why must you always play these games, Viktor? You know I'll get what we *both* want in the end."

"And what is that?" I demand, already knowing the answer.

He advances again, and this time, I allow him to push me backwards, my spine crashing against the fridge door. He restrains my arms by my sides, and the need to fight against the hold sizzles under my skin. His crystal blue eyes bore into mine, wanting permission—and that's where we differ.

I don't ask for things.

I take.

Leaning into him, I let him feel the hard ridges of my cock against his, then force him away from me with a thrust.

A girl who's only been working here a few months enters carrying a tray of empty plates. Her feet stutter to a stop when she sees me. She gives me those doe eyes every time our paths cross and I know her cunt is dripping, wanting me to relieve her ache. I'm a good-looking man. My father always told me our mother passed down her only good gene to us: her looks. I've seen pictures of her. She has the same dark brown hair as me. The same fiery blaze within her honey eyes. My features are slightly softer than Vlad's because I resemble her most.

She left when I was a boy. I hardly remember her at all. Our father doesn't speak of her often, and when he does, they're hateful words spewed out in anger and pain. She is the only weakness I've ever seen him have.

Niko follows my stare and growls for her to leave.

Her eyes widen and her gaze darts between us before dropping to my crotch. My hard cock protrudes against the zipper. The plates clatter when she hurries to place the tray down.

"Vika," I call, stopping her in her tracks before she can flee. I only remember her name because it's the same as our sister's. Two Vikas under one roof. One a shy, poor maid. The other an outgoing, spoiled rich girl. They couldn't be more opposite if they tried. Her big, expressive brown eyes lift to mine, and I summon her with a crook of my finger. "Come here."

"Don't play games that will end badly," Niko warns me.

But that's the point. The dark parts of him are what I like, and I welcome the outcome. I fucking crave it.

Grabbing her by the shoulders, I spin her so her back is to me and she's facing Niko. I take a knee behind her and lift her skirt. She gasps at my bold action. Her panties are black lace, not the cotton I'd thought she'd wear. Satisfied with this little surprise, I pull the fabric aside, and a sprinkling of curly hair strokes across my fingers. And like I predicted, her cunt is dripping and needy. They always are when it comes to me.

I slip two fingers inside, pushing past her lips, and the muscles tighten against them. She doesn't protest like I wish she would.

"You're surprisingly tight, Vika. How many lovers have you taken?"

She groans as I begin a slow tortuous finger-fuck. "Two," she breathes.

Not likely.

"Liar," I tease, leaning to the side to get a good look at the blazing anger on Niko's face.

He doesn't disappoint. His jaw is gritted so tight, the muscles tick. I watch with amusement as his fist clenches and unclenches.

This will teach you for playing games with me, asshole. I'm no one's fool.

"How many really?" I ask as I finger her, my breath

hot against her back.

"Four," she breathes. "Only four. I swear it." Her hands ball up her own dress to give me better access. Little whore.

"I think I'm going to fuck you, Vika. Right here where we make food, then keep you in my room for when I want to play with you again."

She's gasping, her body leaning forward as she attempts to grind herself against my long fingers. I'm so focused on Niko's growls of fury, I miss the moment he snaps. He reaches out for her, but it's so quick, I don't have time to react.

Crack!

The maid stops gyrating immediately and falls forward, limp. Her body slides from my fingers and she hits the floor with a sickening thud.

"You can keep her if you like the smell of rotten corpses," Niko spits out, venom in his words.

He killed her.

"You fucking idiot," I bark. "My father won't like this!"

But I do. Fuck yeah, I do.

"I'll get rid of her," he mutters. "He won't need to know." His face pales as realization of what he's just done sinks in. Killing people isn't new to either of us, but my father has strict rules that allow him to remain as powerful as he is.

Don't kill on impulse. It could come with consequences.

In order to keep the respect, you have to show it.

Killing one of his service maids because you're jealous and can't admit it is a dangerous game no one can win when it comes to my father.

"The cameras would have seen her enter here," I snap. "You can't sweep this under the rug, Niko."

Picking the tray up she discarded, I send it skittering to the floor, the plates shattering and the sound piercing the air. Niko's eyes expand and then narrow, looking between the mess and the door before fixating on me.

Reaching down without breaking his gaze, I lift the girl. Her feet drag along the tiles as I move her across the room and add her to the pile of shattered china. I bend over her lifeless body and pick up a shard from the plate before burrowing it in her neck, relishing in the pop of her skin as it breaks under the force of my hand like biting into a ripe plum. A shiver races up my spine and every hair stands up in attention.

"Clumsiness will get you a knife in the eye or a plate in the neck," I murmur, rolling my shoulders.

Righting myself, I take deliberate strides toward Niko. His skin flushes. He can see the darkness inside me and has always believed it was he who woke the demon. But he doesn't realize my demons have run amuck long before I showed them to him.

His hand reaches out toward me, and I grasp him around the wrist, twisting his arm up his back and forcing him face-down over the counter. My still-hard cock presses into the crease of his ass. "Look what we did," I taunt as I motion at the way the blood blossoms from the wound in her neck. She must still be warm to have a crimson flow seeping from her.

Beautiful.

"You shouldn't tease a monster," Niko growls, wiggling in attempt to free himself.

"There's a flaw in your DNA for sure, but a *monster*?" I chuckle darkly at him. "A *monster*, you are not."

I release his hand, and it slaps down on the counter, but he doesn't try to move or flee. Roughly, I shove his jeans down his thighs, then spit into my palm, barely taking the time to coat the tip of my cock before I take joy in brutalizing him. The roar that rips from him is very monstrous indeed as I ram my cock deep inside his ass. I hope it hurts. *I hope it fucking hurts.* The grunts coming from him indicates it does.

"Fuck you," he rumbles.

How ironic.

"I'm the master here, Niko," I taunt, thrusting my hips forward. "Don't ever forget that."

Heavy boots pound from the corridor and Niko begins to panic, hissing under his breath. "Get off me, Viktor. Someone is coming." I like the way he struggles against me. It makes me want to fuck him harder. So I do.

"Yes, me. I'll be coming if you keep squeezing my cock like that," I tease, pushing in deeper. The entry was tight, pushing past the ringed muscles, but unlucky for Niko, I like pain with my sex—and danger. He doesn't have a choice whether he does or not.

"Viktor," he begs, his voice hoarse.

I chuckle, pulling out of him but not releasing him. Grabbing the back of his neck, I guide him on unsteady feet over to one of the store cupboards, then shove him inside and follow behind, closing us in.

"I missed you," he breathes, his glimpse of vulnerability one I'd like to devour.

"Prove it." I push him down to his knees, my cock

hard and free from our fucking moments before.

He greedily takes me into his mouth, slurping down my cock like it's an ice cream cone and he's overheating.

Yeah, suck down your master's cock. Just like that.

The kitchen door opens and a rumbling of curses sound out from one of my father's men. Other boots and voices join in, and Niko pulls back. Grabbing the back of his head, I force my cock down the back of his throat once more and punish him with my hips. Through the slats on the cupboard door, I watch as two men carry poor, slutty Vika out the back entrance. Another sweeps up the china and mops the floor like it never happened.

No questions.

No tears.

No fucks given.

I pump my hips against Niko's face, savoring the moans vibrating over the supple ridges along my shaft. His mouth sucks strong and fast, his tongue skimming over the helmet. Over and over, his needy mouth moves.

Heat spreads up my spine and tightens my balls as pleasure seeps from my tip down his greedy gullet.

Pulling free just in time, I pump the last drops of my essence over his lips, knowing the sting it will cause to the cut I gave him earlier. He winces slightly, but takes it nonetheless.

The moment I'm drained of all pleasure, I tuck myself away and leave him on his knees. I push open the cupboard doors and stroll back to the meat I dropped on the floor near the refrigerator before scooping it up and throwing it in the bin. The doors open and screeching makes me startle.

"Viktor!" my little sister exclaims, throwing her arms around my neck and kissing over my face.

"Vika." I smile against her cheek. The real Vika. The living Vika. My twin. She's a lot shorter than me, her feet dangling as my neck carries her weight.

Vlad joins us with a rare, honest smile touching his lips. "Surprise." He gestures with open palms, referring to our sister hanging from me like a monkey.

"Indeed," I agree with a raised brow.

"I'm starving," she announces, finally dropping to her feet and freeing me. She weighs nothing, her waist trimmer than it was a month ago.

"You're skin and bones, little sister," I point out.

Her hands drop to her hips and her nose scrunches. Every time I see her, she wears a different hairstyle. This one suits her well. It's short in the back and cut bluntly longer in the front. "One minute does not constitute me being your *little* sister, Viktor. No matter how tall you grow." Her amber eyes twinkle in amusement.

Vlad wraps an arm across her shoulders, tucking her under his armpit. "I've never known twins so opposite as the two of you."

We're not entirely different it would seem.

The cupboard door opens and Niko appears carrying a packet of cookies.

"Niko!" Vika bellows. "I wondered where you disappeared to."

He strolls over to her, a warm smile on his face, and wraps his arms around her. Vlad glares at him.

Vlad and Niko were once best friends, but things have been tense ever since Vika announced she and Niko were in love.

"Oh, there's where your boyfriend went to hide," Vlad grits out.

Reaching up on her tiptoes, Vika plants a kiss to Niko's lips, her face scrunching up. "What have you been eating? You taste delicious."

My cock, little sister.

I have to bite down on my tongue to prevent the snort wanting to rip from me.

"Viktor," my brother barks. "Come. I have something to show you, and if I have to witness that fucker kissing on my baby sister where I eat my breakfast, I may have to kill him…or myself."

I'm right there with you, brother.

Although, I'd always choose his death over mine.

CHAPTER TWO

~ *Defective* ~

Tanner/Cassian/Viktor
Present

K AMI. In my frantic haste to find her, I ignored the dangers of the monster's lair. I exploded into the space in hopes to rescue one of the few links to my past. And it's cost me dearly. Benjamin, emerging from the shadows behind me, shoves me hard, and I deserve it. I deserve the sudden imprisonment. My friend has betrayed me and forced me into a cell beside Kami's.

Fuck.

Strong, fierce, beautiful Kami.

The lioness is nothing more than barely breathing kitty roadkill. A victim. A player very quickly losing this game.

"Kami." My voice breaks, and I fucking hate it. If my brother were here, he'd growl and tell me my mask has slipped. The goddamn poker face has faltered. Such a mistake could mean the difference between life and death. I know this.

But no matter how hard I desperately try to pull it back into place, I can't. Not now. Not after Benjamin. He's not like the others. The man—no, the monster—has always been a gasoline-soaked match just waiting to ignite.

Now he's motherfucking burning.

The flames of rage in his brown eyes show no signs of flickering or dimming. They're out of control. The beast has been unleashed.

We face off—two animals with the same taste for violence.

"You can watch your precious Kami all you want now," he bites out, a smug satisfactory look crossing over his features.

I fucked up.

Benjamin isn't one you turn your back on. Ever. Yet, I did. I let my stupid fucking heart guide me for once. With Kami, the feelings I have for her are almost the same protective feelings I once had for my sister. Although, if Vika were here right now, I doubt I'd find one ounce of the brotherly love for her. Vika tore me in half, and it was Kami who sewed me back together. She replaced the pain inside me with sex and viciousness.

I let her down.

I let him down.

Smashing my fist against the unbreakable Plexiglass, I snarl, "Don't do this, Benjamin. I gave you everything." My chest heaves with exertion.

A pained expression crosses over his features. His vulnerability—despite only ever coming in flashes—is something I've craved from the get-go. An attraction, if you will. A desire to pick through his mental wounds and pluck out the things that eat at him. To implant myself right smack in the middle. To fucking own.

"But it wasn't free, was it?" he demands, his bearded jaw clenching. "It was all a game to you, and it comes at a cost."

My gaze skirts over to Kami, who lies unconscious—at least I hope she's not fucking dead—in her cell. I turn my attention back to him. "Why hurt Kami?" My voice shakes again, and I want to cut my own heart out so I can stomp on it. "Did you—"

"Rape her?" His smile is positively wicked. Delicious. Even under the toe of his proverbial boot, I can appreciate his dark beauty. "She was the price. Your debt. You thought you could play with my doll and I'd allow it? You know me better than that."

And I do.

His dolls are the cross he bears. We all have something we carry. I was careless. It was almost as though I wanted him to discover how a master watches his monster. To delight in the way he'd explode. But now that he's an inferno and I'm trapped in a plastic box, my decision feels stupid.

A wrong move.

Benjamin plays *the game* well. Sometimes, better than I. It's why I befriended him in the first place. Knowing his potential—even before he did—gave me power and a strategy that worked for a little while.

"I helped you with her!" I snap, driving home the reminder that I am the reason he has this whole life in the first place.

His nostrils flare and his hands curl into fists. "By spying on me? By fucking interfering? What about the gifts and notes? The disgusting comments on her page?

Did you think I wouldn't know it was you?" His screams echo off the tiled walls. "I had your man Luke trace the IP address." He snatches an iPad and pushes it against the cell to show me. "It traced back to the club. To you!"

And this is why I'll always beat Benjamin. My monster. My little pet. Because I pay attention to all the moves of *all* the players.

My lip curls up as I shake with anger. "That's not mine, Monster."

Shock skitters across his features. "W-What?"

"Had you not gone all Hulk on me, beat up my friend, and trapped me in this goddamn cage, I'd have had a moment to tell you someone was stalking your pretty new doll, Benjamin," I spit out each word, reveling in the way his eyes blink in confusion.

I'm so sorry, Monster, but you've been played.

"What the fuck are you talking about?" he seethes.

I sit on my ass in the cramped quarters and lean back against the wall. I'm already drenched in sweat and I've been here all of five minutes. This game is going to be tricky.

I've played far worse.

"Not so fast, Benjamin. You're going to calm your ass down first. You will release me from this cage and let me see to Kami. Then, we'll talk."

He snarls, the thick vein on his neck bulging. "You'll talk now or I'll scalp your dumb bitch right here!"

My mask is back in place. Benjamin is violent, but he's also been under my care for three years. I've taught him a lot. Making hasty decisions is frowned upon. The education of Benjamin Stanton was the same one my brother and father taught me.

"You will calm down," I tell him in a bland tone. "You'll calm down because you need me. Yes, I admit, I violated your trust by watching over you. But did you ever fucking consider it's because you're my best friend? That I don't trust a random dolly not to fuck you over? You're mine to look after."

Benjamin falters for a moment, indecision flickering in his eyes. "Who was it?" His tone is deceptively quiet.

"Let me see to Kami, then I'll tell you." I shrug out of my jacket, banging my elbows in the process. He stalks back and forth in front of the cages, slapping at his head. I know he goes a bit mad from time to time. It's me who always brings him back. I *will* bring him back. I toss my tie and start unbuttoning my dress shirt as he stops pacing. His dark eyes bore holes into me.

"What's with the fucking suits all the time?" he demands.

What an unusual question so late in the game. I peel off the sweat-soaked shirt and drop it to the floor.

"All part of the game, Benjamin."

The chaos tending to disturb his mind from time to time has quieted. He towers over my cage, his arms folded across his massive chest. It's as though he's a vengeful god—a god *I* created. And what does that make me? The ultimate master.

"Let me out," I say in a calm manner that usually works on him when he's all raged out. "We'll figure this out together."

And we will. We have to. The thought of this being it—the fucking end between us—is inconceivable.

"Why do you care so much about her?" he demands, his voice shaky, his truth bleeding through. He's hurt because of Kami. Fuck, this is complicated.

All the best games worth playing are…

"She and I go way back," I tell him honestly. "She's like a sister to me."

He smirks, the fury momentarily taking a backseat. "You like the idea of fucking your sister?"

Actually, the idea makes me mental. There are many, many things I want to do to Vika. Cut her throat. Disembowel her. Rip her fucking heart out like she did mine. Sex is the last thing I want to do with her.

"I hate my sister." I let the abhorrence trickle out into my words. If I want Benjamin to let me out of this cage, I need to give him these morsels of the truth. I need him to trust me again.

His dark brows furl together and he steps back like I've struck him. "Why?"

"She betrayed me," I grit out, my gaze darting to Kami.

"Why haven't you ever told me you had a sister?" Again, there's accusation in his tone.

"Because I can't even say her name without wanting to strangle everyone in the room. She's in the past, Benjamin. Just like this little blip in our friendship. I fucked up. But I can help you find your doll's stalker. Together, we can kill that vile human."

Reaching into his pocket, he retrieves his keys, his nostrils flaring as he unlocks Kami's cage. Then, he unlocks mine. "Check on the cunt, then you tell me everything you know."

I could overpower him. It would be tricky because he's so violent and powerful, but I'm cunning and quick. I could do it. However, I'm playing a bigger game. One where my precious monster doesn't die today.

I push open the cell door and crawl out. When I stand, we're a mere six inches apart. Benny and I are evenly matched in height and build. Often, I've had fantasies of pushing him over my desk and fucking him like I used to with Niko. But Benny is such a rare beast, I've spent a lot of time domesticating his animal. One day, he's going to want everything I offer him. Everything.

"I'm sorry, Monster," I tell him, my tone genuine.

He blinks rapidly at me. "Check on her," he barks.

I'm not dead yet, so this is progress. Benjamin tends to act first, think later. The fact that he's thinking—plotting, planning, playing the game—has pride thundering in my chest.

Breaking the spell, I pull away from our intense stare and open Kami's cage. She's breathing softly, so at least she's still alive. Her feet lie at strange angles. He's broken her ankles it would appear. Dark, ugly bruises mottle the flesh.

It wouldn't be the first time she's gotten hurt this badly.

Blood coats the cell floor. Beautiful ruby slits are raised all over the soft pale flesh of her back. I'm so angry for what he's done to her knowing she means something to me. Though, Monster has captivated me with such an intense force, I'm more pissed I missed him doing it. He's inside me.

Poor Kami. My thoughts betray you.

"Kami," I mutter as I push the hair away from her face.

She lets out a ragged sigh and cracks her eyes open through the congealed blood crusting her eyelashes. "Viktor?"

I tense my shoulders at her using my given name. It's been so long since I've heard it pass her lips. Forbidden. The cracking of Benjamin's neck behind me lets me know he heard. Ignoring that for now, I run my thumb across her busted lip.

"How are you feeling?"

She whimpers. "Been better."

"You look like shit," I admit with a laugh. Her wounds are superficial, painful, but she will heal.

"Feel like it too. Ya roigrala etu igru." *I lost this game*, she whispers for only my ears.

Benny slams his fist down on the front of her cage. "You've checked on her. Now tell me, goddammit. Who's been stalking Bethany!"

Kami's eyes widen, fear flashing in her pretty eyes. I hate the look on her. She's always so brave and fierce. It's been engrained in her since birth. Why is she giving up so easily?

I found out Lucy had been using my company system to hack through my networks and computers when the IP address for a client on Elizabeth's site led back to my fucking club.

Lucy had been with me a long fucking time, and loyal to a fault, so her betrayal stung more than I'd ever like to feel for someone so worthless.

She deserves my wrath more than Monster's. Together

would be ideal, but I'm not sure he's willing to play with me any longer.

"It was Lucy," I snap over my shoulder. "Now, are you going to let me stay out of the cage so I can do my damn job to help you?"

Fuck, I hate when my mask slips around Benny. Sometimes I let it slip on purpose. The motherfucking glee in his eyes when I do is all the power I need to know he gets off on it.

Confusion creases his brow as a million questions seemingly battle inside his head. "I hate that cunt. I'm going to fucking kill her." The evil glint in his dark eyes promises just that. His jaw clenches. "If you want me to trust you, Tanner, or Cassian, or fucking Viktor, then you need to start showing me where your loyalty truly lies. Right now, I feel like you see me as your fucking puppet, for you to pull and tighten the strings as you see fit." His muscles pull taunt under the tanned tattooed skin, as if it's his demons moving through his blood.

"I've always been loyal to you, Benjamin. It's Monster and Master. You know this. You feel it."

I'm showing him my vulnerability. He's a weakness in my shield, but he needs to see what this is. What we are. I didn't play him.

"I want to strip Lucy layer by layer for what she has done," I growl. "She infiltrated my network to set me up. Let me have my vengeance too. We can gut the bitch together."

His nostrils flare, the black of his pupils expanding and swallowing any speck of color. Twisting his lips into a snarl, he nods down at Kami.

"Until then, I want you to show me it's Monster and Master like you say. Hurt *this* bitch for *me*." He says *me* like a caress. It would be a gift to him in his eyes.

I clench my jaw, knowing what I must do to earn his trust. Without hesitation, I snag Kami's wrist and jerk her into a sitting position. My eyes meet hers for a moment, and I implore her to understand. The instant I think she gets my message, I twist her hand hard.

A bloodcurdling scream fills the air. Now, seemingly afraid of me, Kami leans away from me, jerking her injured hand toward her chest.

"Ublyudok," she pants. And she's right, I am a bastard.

But I broke the wrist on her right. She's dominant with her left. There was some leniency shown in my move, and it's not the first time I've broken something of hers. She'll get over it. She always does.

Benny growls, but it's one of approval. I scoot out of the cage, then slam the door shut. She gapes at me as I lock the cage back, venom in her stare. Rising, I walk straight up to Benny. His gaze drops to my bare chest, curiosity dancing in his eyes. I've always been careful around him. Dangling the mystery in front of him like a tasty treat for a puppy. He's so hungry for it.

Our eyes lock for a heated stare. Benny's not gay, but neither am I. I'm just a very sexual person. I've been attracted to both males and females. It has nothing to do with what's between their legs and everything to do with what's inside their skull.

If I think it'll be a challenge to possess them, I want them with every ounce of my being.

Benjamin Stanton is the most difficult of them all.

Which means he gets my dick very hard.

With alarming speed, he jerks me around and shoves me against the outer cage door I just occupied. He's fucking strong in his monstrous state, easily able to pin me. I want to go wild and crush my fist through his nose at the thought of being owned when I'm used to doing all the owning. But then his stone-hard erection presses into my ass.

Is this how Niko felt when I'd exert my power of him?

A tiny thrill shoots through me and my own cock stirs.

"Is this what you want?" he snarls, the taunt hateful. "For me to rape you?" He rubs himself against me—one of his power moves. Again, there's that gleam in his eyes whenever he uses my sexuality over me. But he doesn't realize he's slowly beginning to like our sexual charge. He may not understand it, but he likes it. His cock is hard for me. The desire swims in his eyes at times for me. It's always been just a matter of time before I'll win this little game with him and show him what it's like to fuck a god.

"We make a good team," I grit out, the urge to fist my cock overwhelming.

"I want you to lure Lucy here so I can crush her windpipe with my bare hands," he snarls. "Make it happen. And then, I want to get my doll back here so I can put my dick inside her. You want to watch so fucking badly, you're going to watch. I'll put you back in this cage and fuck her right against the glass like this." He thunders his hips against me, his cock mashing painfully against my ass.

Benny and I both know he would never share his precious dolly.

It's as though he's convinced himself the reason I did it was because I'm a pervert dead set on watching him fuck her. But I know him. He'd carve my eyeballs out with a spoon before he let me be a voyeur to them.

"I never cared about seeing *her*," I utter, my voice low with insinuation. "You know who I wanted to watch."

His cock thumps against my ass, and I fight off a triumphant smile. With a growl, he releases me and jerks away. "Make it happen. Get Lucy here."

I turn around to make sure he sees my own hard-on. To let him know he has some sexual power over me. I need for him to see this so we can slip back into our dominant roles of master and monster. His gaze drops for a second before he pins me with a glare.

"Now, *Viktor*." He growls with another wicked gleam in his eyes.

I yank my phone from the pocket of my slacks and dial Lucy. She doesn't answer, so I leave her a message.

"Something important has come up and we need to talk. Meet me in an hour at the club," I say for the recording, my voice calm, not wanting to alert her.

I hang up and level Benny with a hard stare. "I'll get ahold of Lucy, then I'll let you do whatever it is you want to do to her. Master takes care of Monster."

A flicker of relief dances in his stormy eyes.

I'm just about to speak when my phone buzzes. As soon as I see the picture, my chest tightens. This game just got a whole lot more complicated.

"Fuck," I hiss, fury at Lucy threatening to consume me.

Benny's scowl is murderous and the vein in his neck

throbs. "What is it?"

With an irritated sigh, I turn my phone toward him to show him the picture of Elizabeth Stanton—his Bethany doll—tied up naked to a chair. Her mark that Benny created on her chest weeping blood. It should read,

Benny's Doll.

Lucy, the woman with a death wish, has cut through his name and carved a new word above that one.

My Doll.

Here I thought the game was getting close to ending. There are more players than I anticipated. Smart, cunning, vicious players.

The game is just getting started.

An animalistic roar from the beast before me signifies it's most definitely just begun.

CHAPTER THREE

~ *Cracked* ~

Benny

*T*HUD.
    Thud.
Thud.

A roar rips from my ribcage, pulling and snapping tendons. Every muscle tightens and flexes, the skin-stretching taut over them. This vibrating intensity thunders through my veins and settles in my chest. I swear, I can see the fucking heart I let feel again beat from the cage containing it.

Black clouds roll into my thoughts and acid rain pelts down through the marrow of my being, corroding and destroying all rationality. Rage, blinding and terrifying, takes hold of me, igniting into an inferno of inescapable wrath. I rush Tanner, snatching the cell phone from him, and stare down at my Bethany.

This can't be real.

She's mine.

She's fucking mine.

How dare Lucy touch her. Carve into her perfect skin. It's mine to blemish. Not hers. She belongs to me.

Static hums in my mind. I want to kill. Maim and destroy. Annihilate. I just found her. Just got her back with me, and this nobody sadistic freak thinks she can play games with me? *Me!*

"Listen, Benjamin." Tanner, or Viktor, or whoever the fuck he is, tries to placate me. Does he not see the dragon is about to breathe fucking fire?

Grabbing him around the throat, I force his head back against the glass of his cage.

"Is she working under your command?" I will open him up from gullet to groin if this is him playing me.

What a shame that would be.

His eyes narrow and there's something in them. Hurt maybe. Well, fuck him. His blade bitch has my Bethany. "She fucked us both," he growls.

Why is the question. Why the hell would she want my doll?

"Where would she go?" An unexplainable blanket of calm shrouds me. Every emotion ripping through me shrinks into an explosive vault that I push down into my soul. I *need* to focus. I have to get her back. Tanner has taught me many things over the years, and losing your mind in a moment of chaos is the worst thing you can do.

Tanner's eyes flare with uncertainty, the façade he hides behind so well slipping more and more in my company. "We need to check the cameras, and I have everyone tracked. Cells. Cars. Necks," he answers coolly. Of course he fucking does. My eyes flare in warning, and he shakes his head.

"Your neck doesn't have a tracker," he confirms. I guess he gets to be a free dolly…for now. "We need to go to the club." The nagging voices keep tapping at my skull to speak, to encourage me to let the rage out, but if I do, I'll lose myself to it, then lose her because of it.

I want to rampage and kill every living thing on this earth so there's not a single threat to my doll.

My fucking doll.

"If you play me in anyway, I won't go for caging you next time," I snarl, my voice low and deadly. "I will bleed you out instead, then split your Kami straight up the fucking center with a hacksaw and hang her from the entrance of your damn club for all to see what a gaping cunt she is."

"Are we not friends, Benjamin?" he asks me, a sadness in his tone I've never heard before.

"I don't know, *Tanner*, are we?"

His features grow stormy. "We are. And since we're friends, no more secrets. My given name is Viktor. It's what my friends called me back home."

A soft voice calls from next to him, and my eyes drag over to the cop bitch I took earlier.

She's scrambling, trying to get to her feet. "Oh crap," she groans. "I knew you two were freaking weird. Detective Scott is going to have my ass."

She's too flippant for someone locked in a fucking cage with a monster prowling outside. Two long strides and I'm in front of her, my breath misting the glass in wake of my heavy exhales.

"What makes you think Detective Shit Face is going to get anywhere near that ass? Do you not see where you are?" I roar.

She glances between Viktor and I before muttering a string of curse words under her breath. I didn't really pay her much attention before, but now, close-up, the youthfulness of her skin and her unsure stance becomes obvious. Her gaze falls to Kami two cells over. I like this whole glass thing. They can see the brutality of my wrath when they disobey and are bad dollies.

Kami looks like she's on the brink of passing out, and I relish that sting she must have felt deep in her soul when her precious Viktor betrayed her.

"Is she dead?" Cop Doll whispers, her arms wrapping around her waist as the true realization of what she's in for settles into her bones. "Fuck, fuck, fuck, I should have listened and kept my nose out of it."

My fist hammers on the cage. I don't have time for some ditzy bitch to have a panic attack on me. I need to get to Bethany. I could take some of my aggression out on this bitch. Make her bleed, then dump her body at Dillon's feet as a "fuck you" on the way out of town once I have my doll back.

"You don't act like a detective," Viktor pipes up, his gaze probing and assessing. Always the calculating one, *my friend*.

She bites down on her lip and brushes some stray hairs from her face. "I'm not a detective." She shakes her head. "Not yet, anyhow." Then, a shrug. She says it like there's a chance she'll be leaving here. Do I give off a unicorn vibe? Like this is a fucking vacation home?

"If you don't explain further, I'm going to lose my temper and end up using your head as a basketball. How many times do you think I could bounce you before your fucking skull pops?" I growl, my patience wearing thin.

"That's terrifying," she states with a curl of her lip.

"And gross."

What the fuck? I've slipped into the twilight zone.

"Dillon," Viktor barks, interrupting this obnoxious exchange. "Who are you to him?"

She's still frowning at me as she answers him. "No one. Well…I'm his partner's responsibility. He was just showing me the ropes and I got carried away. I thought I could help."

I slam my palm down to stop her annoying chatter. "And look where it got you." I smirk, hoping I look evil as fuck doing it.

Another dimwitted detective they're training.

"I sent him pictures of you." She raises a brow. A "fuck you" if I ever saw one. I thought my dirty doll had balls. This one's are pretty fucking big.

"You're lying," I grate out.

How would she have done that? She couldn't have. Stupid doll.

"When I was at the club and you two were arguing. He will know you have me. Everything will be okay." She's trying to reassure herself, and in doing so, she's poking the fucking giant hungry beast in front of her.

If Dillon knows I'm alive, my life just got ten times more complicated.

Bethany.

Fuck, I don't have time for this.

I snag the keys and unlock her cell door. She backs up as far into the corner as she can.

"Nothing to say now?" I snarl as I approach.

"Benjamin, she could prove useful," Viktor says in that cool, level tone of his. "Let's go. We're wasting time."

He jerks his head, gesturing for us to leave.

What use could she possibly be to me?

I reach toward her, and she flinches. The beast beneath my skin roars with power. Savagely, I tear at her clothes. She begins to cry, soft and pitiful. It's music to my goddamn ears.

"Please don't. Please don't," she begs as I strip her down to her white grandma panties. She isn't wearing a bra, but instead has her tits wrapped in a bandage. Why?

"What's that for?"

She's glaring at me, and I almost want her to fight back.

"I don't like having breasts," she mumbles.

"I could relieve you of them if you'd like?" I grin, pulling my blade from my boot.

"Monster, Bethany is suffering while we're delaying. Come," Viktor demands, and he's right. This will have to wait.

I back out of her cage and slam the door, locking it back up. "Clothes are a privilege, Cop Doll. I'll let you know if you ever earn the right to wear them again."

She doesn't respond. I don't expect her to.

Slipping back into his shirt and grabbing his jacket, Victor's eyes train on Kami, who has wiggled herself up into less of a slouch.

"Cassian," she wheezes, her eyes widening as he begins backing toward the doorway. She already fucked up and told me his real name. No tricking me now. Stupid cunt.

"Don't you dare leave me in here, Cass," she begins, tears leaking from her eyes. I want to cum all over the glass at the sight of them.

He is my *fucking doll, you broken, used-up whore.*

Master bows for one.

Me.

"Viktor," she chokes out, once again using his real name, her sobs overwhelming her. But he's already leading the way out of the bunker. With everything that's been exchanged between us, I'm not one hundred percent sure I should trust him. However, I don't have any choice right now. This wasn't how the day was supposed to pan out. Bethany and I were supposed to be the ones on the road together. To start a new life.

Slipping into the car, Viktor checks his appearance in the vanity mirror over his sunshade, then looks over to me. "You loosened a tooth."

"Is that all?" I scoff. He's fucking lucky.

The name Kami called him still rattles around inside my skull, questions dancing around because of it. Viktor. I've never heard that one before, and she used a thick accent when calling him it.

"So, Viktor, huh?" I ask him. "Sounds foreign."

His jaw tightens. The air around us thickens and closes in until it's too hard to take a breath. I have to open the window to relieve the tension.

"My birth name is Viktor Vasiliev," he says, finally. "When I moved here, I was given the name Cassian Harris. A whole record was made for me. To make me a United States citizen."

A United States citizen?

"You're not American? Where are you from?"

He appears to ponder my question, and I study him

for the answer, to catch him in any lies. "Russia," he finally announces on an exhale. Like he's just lifted a giant boulder from his shoulders.

What the fuck?

He doesn't sound Russian. Not even a little.

"I know what you're thinking, and it's because a speech therapist taught us from a young age how to speak without our accents. *Father* required it. I've lived here a long time, and the accent came easy with time." He grunts and looks down at his hands, flexing them. I can tell he doesn't like his father. I can fucking relate.

"He always said it was a weakness knowing so much about a man just from their accent, so we were taught not to have one."

My heart races. Who the hell are *we*? The sister he spoke of earlier?

"And," I bite out harshly, irritated he's giving me bit by bit. A motherfucking tease.

His eyes close briefly. Does this sister evoke so much pain in him? What did she do to him?

"My brother and sister. There is so much about me I couldn't divulge to you," he says softly. "It's another life. One I've not been a part of for a long time."

"Tell me why you hate your sister," I push. I can see the ache, the betrayal. It saturates him, stripping him of all his color.

How bad must it have been to leave a scar so vivid on his soul?

"She killed me," he announces, his tone hard and ice cold. "She fucking killed me."

CHAPTER FOUR

~ *Crushed* ~

Viktor

I DON'T LIKE THE QUESTIONS. The answers bring pain I've worked a lifetime on ebbing. Thoughts of Vlad crash and collide in my mind.

"This is what you wanted, moy brat, to build an empire to rival our father's."

"But I wanted it for him."

"Well, you need to do it for you. *Prove yourself. Show him who you are."*

I did show him. And now look at me. At the mercy of another.

My eyes snap to the flashing lights as we turn in toward the club and creep along the road.

Fuck. Police cars line the parking lot of my club. My fucking life and everything I built is slowly crumbling around me. That stupid detective Benjamin hates so much must have ordered his minions over here when I left him to poke his nose around.

"She did take a photo," Benjamin hisses, rubbing his hands over his face, manic and uncontained.

"Calm down," I order. "Stay in the car. I'm going to

walk the rest of the way."

His head jerks in my direction, but I don't look at him. "Benjamin. Stay here until I return."

Getting out of the car, I walk down toward my club. The overhung clouds close in around me, summoning the storm inside me to the surface. Everything has gone to shit. All I've worked for is swarming in red and blue.

My father would be disappointed. Vlad would be furious if he knew how deep I'd allowed Benny to burrow inside me.

"Affection is one thing, Viktor, but to attach your emotions to another is a dangerous game. When you have a weakness, people will exploit it."

And how right was he? I allowed Kami in too deep, and my monster used her against me. Lured me in through her, and I fucking fell for it. Walked right into the predator's trap as though I was the prey. Yet, once I got there, desperate for the person I thought I wanted, he locked me away, and the only thing I cared about was the loss of *him*.

Rain begins to trickle down from the sky, and I swear my skin sizzles when the drops touch the flesh. *I'm the fucking devil, so it's fitting.* So much anger rages in my blood at witnessing the disrespect to my establishment. This kind of show is just that—a show. It will ruin trust for my clientele and cost me their business.

If this is Dillon Scott playing games, he is going to be so disappointed with the outcome. I do not break. I do not falter. I do not lose. And one thing Benjamin will have to learn: I do not bow to anyone. I'm a Vasiliev.

Reaching the entrance, I'm stopped with a hand to the chest by a uniformed police officer. It surprises me they allowed me to get this close before stopping me, which tells me they have no right to be here. They're just playing scare tactics or a diversion.

"Sir, this establishment is closed until further notice."

"Says who?" I ask, my voice calm, though I feel anything but. Fire blazes inside me, barely controlled.

He seems momentarily surprised by my words, and instead of looking over me like before, he brings his stare down to my face. "Says the county sheriff's department."

"Do you have a warrant?" I narrow my gaze on him and watch the waver in his features.

Yeah, you can wear a uniform, but that won't protect you from beasts like me.

"Samuels," he barks without looking away from me. *Yes, you should keep me in your sights, motherfucker.* "Bring the warrant over here."

"Uh, Dean has it?" someone shouts back.

Wagging my finger in his face, I bite out, "Hmm, you shouldn't play games you can't win. I will have you personally held accountable when I sue the department because we both know you don't have a fucking warrant."

"Ten minutes out, sir," someone calls out, and this asshole in front of me smirks before stepping to the side.

"Enjoy your time at The Vault," he sneers. "Make the most of it."

Pushing past him, I make my way inside. The girls from the front desk rush over to me, but I hold up a hand to stop them from speaking. I don't have time for them right now. If the ten minutes the prick outside was referring to was about them having a warrant here, then I need to work fast.

My office is how I left it, and I'm relieved Detective Scott didn't take my laptop with him. Bringing it to life, Kami once again fills the screen. She must be in so much pain. Deep, soul crushing pain. I'm all she's ever had, and I just cut her deeper than any blade could. She won't forgive lightly for this. My thoughts drift to the past.

"Why are they being held here?" I ask Vlad as he leads me into the basement. Cells line the wall like prison rooms.

"These are payments, forfeits, debts," he calmly states, tapping his hand on each door as we pass it. I've lived in this house my entire life, yet never knew this existed.

"And they're entering The V Games?" I query.

"They are sacrificed for pleasure and entertainment." He stops outside one of the cells and gestures with his head for me to look through the sliver of space left open on the door. Stepping forward, my eyes peek through the slat and fall upon a young girl sitting cross-legged on a cot. Blonde hair curtains around her face, blocking her from view. She's slender, and wearing sweatpants, a sweatshirt, and heavy boots.

"Who is she?"

"She's no one now, but she was once a daughter to a man who owed too much money to our father and couldn't afford his debt," Vlad states, and with his words, they summon the girl to lift her head. She's pretty, but tortured. Her eyes are haunted, and it makes my dick jerk. Her plush, full lips part, and I lean in closer in anticipation of what she's going to say. Crooking a finger, she curls it toward her in a come here motion.

"Why don't you come in and play?" she beckons in English, but with a thick Russian accent. I'm almost trying to magically pass through the steel of the door to get to her when Vlad's laughter resonates around me.

"Don't be fooled by her pretty face, moy brat. She's deadlier than she looks."

What?

Snapping my attention to my brother, my brow furrows. "How so?"

"She's been trained from a young age. She's a fighter. Her name is Klara Alla Mila Ivanov."

My eyes widen. "The girl from the underground Black Circle fights?" *I breathe.*

"One in the same."

She was known for being forced to fight by her father from the age of ten, and gained a reputation through years of defeating opponents in the underground fighting circuit.

"Let her out. I want to see what she has." Energy, wild and erratic, hums in my veins at the thought of getting to spar with her.

"Are you sure? If she beats you, I'll hold it over you for all eternity," Vlad mocks.

"If she beats me, your training methods need improvement, brat," I taunt back.

"Very well."

The clanking of the door disengaging sends my heart rate thundering. The blood rushes through my veins, flooding me with adrenaline.

The door opens and she stands in between the frame, her eyes hooded as she surveys me. Her hands ball into fists, and fresh ink, still red and angry on her wrist, spells her *initials and a barcode beneath it. **K.A.M.I. - 15k000076**.*

Kami.

I like it much better than her given name.

In fact, that is what I'll call her from here on out.

"Play nice. No permanent damage," Vlad warns her, and she smirks up at him.

"How old are you?" I ask, scrutinizing her youthful features. Her soft skin is unblemished. Her nose is crooked where she's taken too many hits, but it doesn't take away from her beauty. Instead, it gives her character.

"Old enough to hurt you," she replies, her tone cold and confident.

I like her.

Vlad was right.

He's always right, although I'd never admit that to his smug ass.

She rushes me, her arms quick to deploy martial arts moves. I block her motions, and she adds some kicks, catching me off guard. She lands a blow to my mouth. Blood blossoms and floods over my tongue from my tooth piercing the gum.

She grins when she sees she's cut me.

Spitting the blood to the floor, I grin back at her before charging and grappling her to the floor. A thud sounds as her head hits the concrete, causing her to cry out in pain. It's brief, and she's soon trying to hit me with her fists. Her legs wrap around my waist and she tries to turn us so she's on top and at an advantage. I'm much stronger than she is, though, and I restrain her by twisting her onto her front and pinning her arms beneath her.

She's lost.

There's nothing she can do from here.

I lean down to her ear and whisper, "I win."

She drops her head, which I think is in defeat, but then she lifts it all too fast, crashing the back of her skull into my nose and knocking me backwards. Bitch.

She squirms her way free as my hands grip my broken nose. Blood seeps through my fingertips and my eyes lift to find Vlad glaring at me.

"You don't celebrate a victory until your opponent is truly defeated," he booms.

"I win," she boasts, coming at me with a boot raised.

I grab her foot and tackle her back to the ground. She struggles, but a closed fist to her face and she's out cold.

"I fucking win," I grind out, pinning my older brother with a glare.

"Good," Vlad states. "Now, put her back in her room and let's go eat."

Every day, we repeat this game until it's time for the real games.

With a shake of my head to clear away the past, I bring up the software for the trackers I have placed on all my close employees. I'm a businessman and no one's fool. All the employees who deal with the less legal parts of my company are tracked so if they ever do break my rules, they can't hide from my fury.

Bad apples must be eliminated so they don't infect others and turn the whole pack sour.

I've never had to implement this before. I am a vicious wolf when it comes to who I allow in the pack, and my team has been with me for decades. Lucy was twenty when I found her. She went by her given name then, Jessica, and had an insatiable fetish for making people bleed, but her skill with a blade needed honing. It took five years before I moved her from the floor of the club to the other side of things. I learned everything about her. She was from right here in this town. Straight A student. But then, everything for her changed. She dropped out of school to run away from home at the young age of sixteen. When I asked her about that time in her life, she gave me a vague answer: *"Life pushed me, but I will push back harder."*

I always found her answer endearing. Vague is how I've always been. It's what keeps me a step above everyone else.

Her parents died over a decade ago in a boating accident and Lucy didn't even blink when I informed her of their passing. She was cold, and I admired her for it. I would never have believed she was capable of betraying me. She worshipped me. Would do anything I asked. And I rewarded her for her idolization by moving her up the ranks.

The penetrating rage swarms around under my skin like a thousand scorpions pinching and snapping at the tendons. If I don't release some of it soon, it's going to consume me and take over.

Disloyalty is my trigger. If there is anything you can do to hurt me, it's betray my trust. My usual invincible façade fractures and shatters when someone gets one over on me. I worked my entire life to build my fortress. My iron castle is impenetrable, yet there were cracks all along.

"You can't let this defeat you. You grow stronger from

it. Learn, adapt, and fucking conquer, Viktor."

Vlad's words before I left to come here anchor me, bringing my attention back to the screen in front of me.

The GPS locator for Lucy's implant is a red blinking dot on the screen in matching rhythm of my pulse.

"Stop what you're doing and move away from the desk, Mr. Harris. Now," Detective Dillon Scott bellows from the doorway.

Motherfucker. He's getting on my last damn nerve.

CHAPTER FIVE

~ Mangled ~

Dillon

THE MOTHERFUCKER STARES AT ME from the back of my cruiser, his amber eyes boring into mine in the mirror. Smug. Cold. Unaffected. I didn't have anything to arrest him on, because quite frankly, I don't have shit yet, but the idiot came willingly when I told him I needed to bring him to the precinct for questioning. And I do. He knows Benny, and I need to know what their relationship is.

Pulling in a favor with the judge to get the search warrant for The Vault so fast wasn't difficult considering what we have in our arsenal: ex police chief, Benny's father, Steve Stanton's brutal murder on the cell phone recovered at the club. A female prisoner slashed up on this jerkoff's computer. And best of all, a photo of the wanted Benny fucking Stanton on the premises. Lucky for me, these idiots lacked a full brain cell between them and the warrant scared them enough to comply.

It's too easy.

I sense Harris isn't going to be forthcoming. He's too smug for someone sitting in the back of a police car, and my hackles are already raised on high alert knowing Benny is lurking out there.

Why hasn't he come for Jade, or attacked me at least?

I don't like any of it.

Feels too easy.

Like I'm missing something.

Right now, though, the only thing that matters is I have Harris's laptop bagged as evidence and one of the uniforms will bring it back to the station. More importantly, I have a key player in this fucked up shit sitting in my backseat. Before we left, I made sure to scour that entire damn club for Benny, but of course he didn't turn up. He's slippery as hell. Cassian Harris is my best lead right now.

He'll lead me to Benny. He has to.

They know each other. Somehow. Some way. I had a hunch this asshole was a bigger player in a game I wasn't quite sure we were playing. When in his presence, there was something about him that bothered me. A nervous energy haunting me. And now I *know* it was Benny. Evil doesn't die that easily, and his scent must have been all over this fucker, waiting for me to sniff him out. The hairs on the back of my neck rise when I glimpse him eyeballing me in the rearview mirror. My gut tells me something lurks under his preppy exterior.

Of course, I never imagined this guy would be in bed with the likes of Benny. Fuck, how do they even know each other? Benny is a loner. I need answers.

The pictures Josey sent were most definitely him. Tattooed. Bearded. Shaved head. But still the same evil. And once I saw those pictures, I immediately realized he was the one I'd seen with Elizabeth that day—just the back of him, but it was him. The bastard was right under my fucking nose and within shooting distance. Kissing. I know now those two were kissing that day, and he's most likely the one who cut her neck, which really stresses me the fuck out. If she's in some relationship with Benny, things just got a hell of a lot weirder. It makes sense, though.

Her doll fetish.

The strange clothes.

She's just like her brother in that aspect. A perversion for that weird shit. I should have seen it much sooner. I should have fucking protected her. And now that's just one more problem on my massive list of shit that's giving me ulcers.

Elizabeth is gone.

I grip the steering wheel so tightly, my knuckles turn white. Cassian Harris continues to stare at me as if he knows every-fucking-thing, and it enrages me. He's about to fucking spill every goddamn bit of it.

"How do you know Benny?" I demand, my voice cold as I drive.

He smirks in the mirror. "I'm not sure I know who you're referring to."

Smug fuck.

"Cut the shit, Harris. You and I both know you're fucking friends with that psycho. He hurt my wife, and I'm afraid he'll hurt someone dear to me as well. Do yourself a favor and tell me everything."

He smiles at me, wolfish and calculating. It makes me want to pull over and slam my fist through his perfect white teeth. "Friends. With a ghost?"

My phone rings, giving me a reprieve from the asshole in my backseat. "Detective Scott," I bark.

"Fuck," Marcus hisses. "This is bad."

My heart thunders in my chest. If Benny has my girls… No, I left them safe at the precinct surrounded by armed officers. "What?" I snap, impatient with his games today.

"An eye witness at Josey's place described Benny to a T. Showed her the photo from what Josey sent us and she confirmed he was the man who took her. *Took*, Dillon. He *took* Josey. It wasn't a break in. It was a kidnapping." His voice cracks as he continues. "He has them fucking both. Elise's sister *and* Josey. Christ. We know what he can do. What he did to Jade…" he trails off, and Elise starts to sob in the background. They're together wherever they are. Under normal circumstances, I'd be giving him hell for that, but right now, I have too much on my plate.

Two missing people—people I know and care about.

And a fucking found person. Benjamin Fucking Stanton.

"Fuck!" I glare at Mr. Harris in the backseat.

"Units are processing the scene for evidence. I'm on my way back to Elise's house to see if I can glean anything from that scene. Detective Rhodes and Sharpton are already there. I feel like this Benny fucker has us stretched out all over the goddamn place," he seethes. "Find anything at the club?"

I dart my eyes to Harris again. "I've got a lead."

He senses the vagueness in my words. "Ahhh. You got the big boss? Bringing him in for questioning?"

"I will get answers," I confirm.

"Good," he barks. "I'll let you know if we find any evidence at the Stanton's."

We hang up as I pull into the parking lot of the precinct. I shut the car off and stare at Harris with venom in my glare. "I don't play games."

"Oh, but *I* do." Another evil smile.

Gritting my teeth, I run my fingers through my hair. "You're protecting that sick fuck for whatever reason. Right now, I'm more concerned about the whereabouts of my friends. Is there anywhere he could have taken them that you know of? I don't think I need to tell you that if you're colluding with him and we find out, you'll be put away for a long time. Accessory to kidnapping…" I trail off, hoping he'll get the impact of my statement.

"Is that all?" His dark eyebrow lifts in amusement. "From what I've been told, this Benjamin character is quite the tyrant. He doesn't seem the type to simply kidnap them. Why do you call him sick? Is there a cure for what he has?"

Flashes of Jade and Macy's old cells flit through my mind. I think about all the murders in Benny's wake. The torment and torture and insanity. This asshole is right. Benny doesn't simply kidnap. He rapes and kills, and there is no cure for his kind of sickness.

Benny is a monster.

"From what I know of the man you speak of, he has ravenous cravings."

"You've made your point," I seethe. "And that is exactly why you need to cooperate with the police."

I'm eager to get inside and check on Jade and MJ. Once I realized Benny was back, I wanted my girls safe.

The precinct is the safest place in the city. Jade doesn't even know about Josey and Elizabeth's apparent kidnappings yet. Rhodes called earlier to tell me they found and bagged Elizabeth's cell phone, but have been unable to trace the number she used to correspond with Benny to anywhere. Another dead end. But she's definitely gone and there was a struggle. The front door was left wide open, her suitcases abandoned in the doorway, and her shoe was on the porch.

Benny has been around this whole time and in our space, yet alluded detection. What if we don't find her and she's left with him for years like Jade and Macy? Bile creeps up my throat, and I choke it down.

"Why is it you think I would help—" he starts, but my heart skips when the back door opens behind me.

My gaze is still fixed on Harris through the mirror when a blade digs into the side of my throat, drawing blood.

Thud.
Thud.
Thud.

I didn't pay enough attention. Underestimated this motherfucker. I know who holds the knife before I angle my head slightly to see who's joined us. When my gaze meets Benny's cold brown eyes, rage threatens to consume me.

It's really him. Knowing and seeing are two different things.

The air thickens and closes in, condensing the small space of the car. My insides squeeze and contort, strangling my lungs so I can't gasp in a full breath.

He's in my car, just feet away from the entrance of the precinct where my family is.

"Fuck!" I snap. Blood slides down the side of my throat, wetting the collar of my white dress shirt. The blade isn't in deep enough to hurt, but it's enough to make a statement.

And knowing Benny's fucked-up state of mind, he could deepen that blade at any point and do it with pleasure in his heart. I can't be taken away from my girls.

"Where is she?" Benny bellows, his eyes manic, red veins running angry across the white, his pupils a black abyss swallowing the brown. I'd die and take him with me before I ever allowed him near my wife again.

My nostrils flare. "You will never lay eyes on Jade again. I will fucking kill you—"

His eyes narrow and his brow collapses. "Not *her*," he snarls. "Bethany."

I blink in confusion. Harris fucking laughs.

Bethany?

"He means Elizabeth Stanton," Harris chimes, tilting his head to the side to study my expression. "His pretty new doll," he adds as a taunt.

My fists curl as furious hate swirls beneath my skin like an entity. It runs through my veins like a fucking jet stream of motherfucking rage. "She. Is. Not. Your. Doll." I'm calculating whether I can get my gun off my belt and shoot Benny in the fucking eye when Harris speaks up. His tone seems to keep Benny from digging the knife further into my neck. They *are* friends.

"Technically, she *was* his doll, then someone stole her," Harris says as he gestures toward the front seat. "If you check my cell phone, you'll see."

Someone stole her, as in someone other than Benny? What the fuck is going on?

Reaching across to the passenger seat where I tossed his belongings while trying not to move my head is harder than it seems. A gasp involuntarily pushes past my lips as the blade slices deeper. Motherfucker. I hold up the cell and Harris lifts his shoulders to signal he can't move. I put cuffs on him to protect myself. My car doesn't have a barrier separating us, and I couldn't risk him becoming brazen and trying to throttle me from behind.

"Keys," Benny growls, his spittle hitting my cheek. He's so fucking close, I can smell the madness on him.

Pulling the keys from my pocket, I offer them over and tighten my jaw. This is not how I thought my day would pan out. Benny's eyes flit over to Harris, who turns for him to un-cuff him. If I'm quick, I could maybe get out of the car. It's a risk, though, and could get bloody if Benny rushes me over the seat.

My decision-making is over sooner than I anticipated when Harris is released and thumbing through his cell phone and Benny's attention is fully back on me.

Great.

He swipes open the phone, then reaches forward to show me a picture.

Thud.

Elizabeth, what the hell happened to you? I gape in horror at the words carved on her naked body.

"W-What the f-fuck is this shit?" I stammer, bile rising in my throat again. Her tiny tits are smeared with blood. Hell, blood is even pooling at the juncture between her thighs. She's just a fucking kid, not some goddamn doll for this sadistic fuck to cut up.

"I swear to Christ, if you don't use that knife to finish me, it's going to be in your dead black heart, you sick motherfucker," I roar. I'm quick, moving to the side, then forward so the knife only nicks me a little. Everything moves in slow motion. Benny's eyes expand as I turn to face him, ripping my gun from my holster as I move.

Thud.

Thud.

Thud.

Noise, loud and distorted, thunders around us like a tropical storm erupting in the small confines.

"I know Jade is here," Benny bellows over the chaos, and the air stiffens. We all stop moving. Hell, maybe stop breathing.

Benny gestures with a nod to the side of the building. Taking a quick glimpse, some big fucker grins back at me.

"He will go inside and alert everyone to what's happening out here and they will all come running, leaving your little family alone and at his mercy. So stop trying to be a hero. You've never fucking been one," he growls, his eyes flitting inside their sockets, the veins underneath bulging. He really is a monster.

"Everyone just needs to take a breath. We all want the same thing." Harris quirks a brow and smirks. He's so calm, it's unsettling.

"She was Benny's doll, but now she's *her* doll. One of my employees took her. My associate here would like his precious dolly back," Harris tells me before waving the horrible fucking image of Elizabeth in my sight.

They want me to believe he doesn't have Elizabeth?

"Why take Josey then?" I snap, my hard gaze meeting Benny's between the gap in the front seats.

"That dumb cop doll was in my fucking way. She stuck her nose in places it shouldn't have been," Benny rages, the knife held out toward me, my own blood dripping from the tip. I wince at the sting in my neck. Jade is going to freak the fuck out when she sees it. "She was nosing around and ruining a good thing between me and my Bethany. Getting you and the other shit pigs on my trail. She needs to be taught a lesson."

"She looked so frightened in her cage," Harris says, egging me the fuck on.

"Enough!" Benny bellows.

"Why are you here then?" I demand. "To take your sick bestie here back home so you two can fuck and kill my friend?" I'm not seeing the whole goddamn picture here.

"She's into chicks, not dicks," Harris pipes up, smirking.

Would that stop Benny?

"We're leaving *together*," Benny snaps. "And you're going to use your police bullshit to find my Bethany!"

"Elizabeth Stanton," Harris clarifies again, and laughs. "Just making sure you can keep up, Detective."

My eyes dart back and forth between these two monsters. One is calculating and calm. The other is unpredictable and feral. Together, they're what motherfucking nightmares are made of.

"What about the female on the monitor?" I ask, recalling the woman who was hurt and seemed to rattle

Harris. "Is she okay?"

"She's none of your concern," Harris bristles, and it's the first time I've seen a dint in his armor.

I scramble for a solution. "Josey. You get me Josey and we'll find Elizabeth. We have a mutual interest, that's for sure." I don't tell him once I find Elizabeth, there's no way in fucking hell Benny will ever touch a hair on her again. "I'll need to question you both—"

"Question time is over, Detective," Harris says, and reaches forward to pluck one of my business cards from the console. "When we have a lead for you to follow like the good fucking dog you are, I'll call you. Until then, I'll be needing my goddamn computer and we're getting the hell out of here."

"I want Josey. Before I even think about helping you find Elizabeth or giving you anything back, I want Josey. That is my deal. Josey, and you get your laptop and my help." I meet both of their cold gazes. I can't believe I'm bargaining with these motherfuckers.

"Tonight."

Benny's eyes narrow. "And I was so looking forward to fucking the unwilling cunt. She'd have screamed so much." Despite his threats, I see a flicker of irritation in his eyes. He doesn't want to fuck her. He wants Elizabeth. For some fucked up reason, he's attached himself to her like he once was with Jade, and I want to know why. He won't ever get her, but he doesn't know that.

"Why Elizabeth? She's your sister. Blood sister. You know that, right?"

"Don't try to make it wrong or perverted. You could never understand. *She* understands me," Benny seethes, his knife twisting a little further in my direction. More blood trickles down my throat, almost in warning. "She loves me. She's mine."

Whatever you say, psycho.

"In two hours. I want Josey in my custody, then we'll find her. Until then, I need to know anyone who could have had a vendetta against you. This isn't a random kidnapping. This person knew where Elizabeth lived. They clearly knew your connection to her based upon that sick fucking picture. I want everything there is to know on this guy."

Harris grips Benny's wrist, gently pulling him away, and it shocks me when Benny complies. Are these two assholes fuckbuddies or some shit? I press my palm to my neck to staunch the bleeding.

"Female. Lucy Vandross is her alias. But look into Jessica Johnson. She's local," Harris says, his voice cool and businesslike. I hate how fucking smug he looks. As if he's the one calling the shots here. And the fact that he has Benny on a tight fucking leash blows my mind.

"Two hours," I snap.

"See you soon, Detective. Don't fuck this up or things could end badly for everyone. And bring my laptop," Harris threatens.

Benny throws open the car door, but not before shooting me a menacing glare. "Tell Jade and MJ I say hi."

They're gone in the next instant, disappearing between cars. I should go after them and be the real fucking cop I am, but I don't.

Benny wants Elizabeth.

He has Josey.

This is the only bargaining chip I have right now, and I sure as hell am going to use it. Fuck protocol. I'm getting my friends back.

Then I'm going to end both those monsters and send them back to hell where they belong. Stepping from the car, I march over to the big guy still standing there smiling at me like we're fucking buddies.

"Great job. It looked totally convincing." He beams.

"What?" I bark out, annoyance making my nerves rattle.

"The scene. That guy paid me to be an extra. I can't even see where the cameras are filming. It's incredible."

"You don't know him or that you're trying to intimidate a police officer?"

His eyes bulge and his skin pales. "What? I was just paid to stand here as an extra."

A decoy. Dumb motherfucker.

CHAPTER SIX

~ Fragmented ~

Elizabeth

Cold.

Dark.

Alone.

I'm not sure how many hours have passed since that crazy blonde woman took me from my house. Two. Maybe three. Long enough for her to cut my clothes right off my body and ruin Benny's work.

She made me cry.

I hate her.

The moment she dug her knife into my stomach and crossed his name out, I broke down. It wasn't that it hurt. It was that I'd finally found some sort of happiness and this bitch was stealing it straight from me. Ruining his mark on me. Taking me from my master.

I wince as I try to sit up on the bed. She has me bound at my wrists, but I'm otherwise free. We're in a dilapidated old motel that smells of mothballs and stale cigarette smoke. The only sound that can be heard is the constant dripping from the bathroom.

Drip.

Drip.

Drip.

One quick glance around the room tells me she isn't here. Lucy is what she told me her name was. But that's all she told me. I've yet to discover, despite all my demands, why she's taken me.

An obsessed fan from my site?

An enemy of Benny's?

I'm not sure.

My gaze continues to scan the space for anything to be of assistance. The phone is just out of re—

Bam!

The motel room door bursts open and slams against the wall. I shriek in surprise. Much to my dismay, it's her, wearing a pair of fitted jeans and a tight white V-neck sweater that shows off her big breasts. Since she ruined her last outfit with my blood, she's taken the time to freshen up. It makes me hate her more. Her perfect blonde hair hangs in waves in front of her shoulders and her makeup is flawless, down to the cat-eye she lined her eyes with. She's older than me, I can tell that much, and there's soft crinkles around her eyes.

Meanwhile, I lie here bloody, beaten, bruised, and disgusting.

Drip.

Drip.

Drip.

"Why am I here?" I demand, my glare focused on her.

She smirks and sits beside me on the bed. I don't trust her smiles or her slow moves. She's like a panther. Deadly and violent. But sleek and beautiful. She's waiting to strike again. I can see it flickering in her eyes. Her palm runs up my naked thigh and her fingertips brush against my blood-crusted pussy.

"I can see why he adores you," she says in a tone that sounds remotely jealous. A fire of irritation blossoms inside me. Does she want him? Does she want my master?

"I can see why he wants to cut your heart out," I throw back at her, my words hateful.

She laughs, and it's throaty. Sexy. Pure woman. I feel as though I'm a dirty little girl in her presence. Have they had sex before? Is she a jealous ex-lover? Anxiety shoots through my veins. I don't like the idea of him with anyone, especially not someone beautiful like her.

"Sweet doll…" She grins and teases my clit with her finger. I squeeze my thighs together to try to stop her from touching what doesn't belong to her.

My body belongs to my brother.

Benjamin.

Master.

"As adorable as you are," she purrs, "you are merely nothing but a useful tool. I'm going to use you so fucking hard to get what I want."

I cry out as she pushes her finger forcefully inside me. I'm dry and sore from when Benny and I had sex. Her intrusion burns, but I refuse to let tears fall. I already gave too many to her earlier.

She pulls her phone from her pocket and snaps a picture of her finger inside me. When she's satisfied, she slides it from my body and sucks on it.

"Mmmm, your pussy is sweet." Her eyes darken as she runs her fingernail along a still bleeding cut on my stomach. "But your blood is sweeter."

When Benny cut and sucked on me, I was into this whole blood play thing. But with her, she's like a fucking vampire dead set on draining me dry. It's disturbing.

"He'll kill you," I threaten. Based on his past and how much he seems to adore me, I hope this is true.

She turns her gaze toward the window. "He's going to try." Her eyes snap back to mine, hate flashing in them. "And that's exactly what I'm hoping for."

A trap.

This bitch is using me to set Benny up.

"If he doesn't kill you, I will," I seethe.

She stands from the bed and walks over to the mirror. Using her wet, still-bloody finger, she writes something on the glass. "You're not capable of such things, sweet doll. Only monsters are. You are *not* a monster."

I clench my teeth and glare at her message in the mirror.

Revenge.

She has no idea. Benny will find me. He won't let this psycho take me…not when we just found each other. I know this with every part of my being. I feel it deep down in my soul.

"You have no idea what I'm capable of," I whisper.

I can be a monster too. It's in our DNA.

CHAPTER SEVEN

~ Ruptured ~

Benny

I MUCH PREFER THE NAME Viktor and feel closer to him now knowing his real name. I don't know why it matters so much, but it does. It just fucking does.

Risking myself to free him from Dillon's shackles was necessary to get the information about his tracking system.

Keep telling yourself that.

"Viktor?" I repeat after asking him what he picked up before the police took everything.

"It showed your sister's home, but she can't be there, and for us to go there is too risky."

"We're going," I state.

What if she's hiding in plain sight or at the neighbors? It's a clever idea.

"Police will be there. It's a crime scene," he almost growls, and my dick twitches at the thought of him losing his cool.

I pull onto the street and point toward the house. "Two cars. Hardly a squad. They're all too busy at your club." I poke the angry bear, willing him to bite back.

His posture stiffens at the mention of The Vault, but he doesn't take the bait.

"I am sorry this shit touched your club. I know how you feel about that place." I contradict my actions with an apology to rock his equilibrium. It sounds sincere, but I'm anything but. I don't actually give a shit about his fucking club or the idiots he caters to there. They tame themselves—hide their desires, their damage. Mine is worn like clothes. It's who I am.

"I know you better than you think, friend. And you don't care about such things." Viktor smirks, tugging at the cuffs of his shirtsleeves. Well, damn. "I need to change." He quivers. His disheveled appearance is wearing on him. If only he knew how good it looked on him, all roughed up and messy. Sometimes us monsters look better free. I'm not sure why he feels the need to contain himself.

"Look. That unit is leaving," I point out as the uniformed officers retreat in their vehicle. "I'm going in."

His hand grasps my forearm. "There're still people in there." A silhouette passes by the window. The heat from Viktor's hold burns, and I'm still not sure how I feel about everything that's transpired between us. It's all hazy in my mind and I can't focus on it right now. I need to find Bethany before that blonde whore does any more damage. I need in this house because there may be clues.

"It's your turn to wait for me and save my ass if I get into trouble," I jest, pushing the door open and climbing from the car.

I hear his door open and his footfalls fall in line next to mine as I cross the street.

"Waiting makes me anxious," he retorts.

He doesn't get anxious.

Creeping up against the side of the house, I peer into the window and see nothing.

"Go around the back. I'll go in the front."

"We shouldn't separate," he whisper-yells after me.

"God, more of you?" some asshole barks from the next door neighbor's yard. "Are you going to be leaving at some point tonight?" He's holding a trash bag in his hand and wearing shorts, socks, and flip flops with no shirt.

"Go back inside, sir," Viktor instructs, authority in his tone—a tone he's used on me more than once. "This is official police business."

"Don't tell me what to do. We've had you guys coming and going all day and night."

His voice is getting louder and will eventually summon whoever is inside if he doesn't shut the fuck up. Sensing my tense posture and glaring eyes, Viktor moves toward the man. I think he's going to walk him inside. He surprises me though, and instead slips his hand into this jacket before launching toward the fuckwit.

Quick, powerful strikes of his wrists, a glint of metal from the car keys in his hand.

One, two, three, four, five, six.

And then he's stepping around him and catching the falling form. Crimson rivers trickle from several little holes in the man's side, a punctured lung so easy. Quick. Beautiful to watch.

The car keys dangle from Viktor's finger, a piece of flesh skewed on the end. The strength he would have had to use is astounding, yet he made it look effortless.

He drags him behind some shrubbery and drops him

without breaking a fucking sweat.

Who's the monster now, Master?

He cracks his neck and brushes down the lapels of his jacket as the side of his mouth curls up. "He gives a whole new meaning to fashion to die for, or because of, in his case. No man should wear socks with flip flops."

"No man should wear flip flops in general," I retort, a smile tugging at my lips. I nod back toward the house. By some miracle, we haven't raised attention. He disappears to the back as I creep up the front.

There are raised voices inside and what sounds like crying. It's familiar.

Pretty new doll.

My feet move without permission, and the next thing I know, I'm inside. The heat of the house engulfs me as two sets of eyes spring to mine.

The sister, not my doll, screams and scurries from her seat toward Dillon's partner.

"Don't fucking move!" he warns, pulling a gun and aiming straight at me. My nerves are so fucking frayed from worrying about my doll, I'm becoming reckless.

Just as I'm trying to contemplate how I can get to him before he gets a shot off, Viktor appears in the doorway behind Elise. He lifts his brow at me and I can read all the words he's not speaking, but conveying perfectly.

"Glad I came now, Monster?"

Fucking right I am. We make quite the team.

He wraps his large palm around my sister's mouth from behind and pulls her body against his. She squirms and kicks back, but he subdues her easily. She's no match for Viktor.

The cop trains his attention on them and I advance on him.

"Don't fucking move," he barks out again, flitting his gaze between the two beasts in the room with him.

"Drop the gun or I'll snap her pretty little neck," Viktor cautions, dropping his hand from her mouth to her neck and squeezing. She makes a weird wailing sound. It's new to my ears and amusing. Her eyes widen and glass over with tears.

"Please don't hurt me. I'm pregnant," she chokes out, and the idiot holding the gun falters, giving me a chance to rush him. My fist collides with his jaw as my arm comes over his, trapping it and taking the gun from him. I smack him with the butt of it for good measure, and he drops like a sack of shit, keeping his unfocused gaze on my doll's sister—*my* sister.

Viktor releases her and points to a chair. "Sit and don't move. If you do, there will be no heartbeats left alive within these walls, let alone the tiny one in your womb."

She's shaking, scared of me—of the both of us—and it's a turn-on. If I squint, she could almost pass for my doll. "Are you here for me?" she croaks, sniffling her snot back up her dripping nose.

Oh, wouldn't you like that? To hold it over my precious new doll that I wanted you? Never, bitch.

"No. I'm here to find Bethany."

Her brows pull together in confusion. Using the palm of her hand, she swipes up her nose, smearing tears and snot everywhere. Wasn't she supposed to be the perfect one? All those people were blinded. They'd been too focused on this fraud when they had something beautiful and real right in front of their noses. My stunning Bethany.

"Who?" She sniffles again.

Viktor exhales hard and runs a hand through his hair. It's become unruly from his day from hell. Very unlike him, but I like it this way. He's coming apart at the seams, and I want to be the one to sew him back together. That's what I do for my dolls. I stitch them back exactly the way I like them.

"He means Elizabeth." He takes a couple strides toward the bleeding son of a bitch on the ground. Dropping to his haunches, he pulls a tissue from a box on the table next to him and dabs at the cop's lip. "You're bleeding," he taunts.

"What evidence did you find here?"

"Fuck you," the idiot spits back.

Wagging his finger and tutting, Viktor stands. "You must be mistaken about the dynamics laid out before you, Detective Marcus James. You see, I know the fetus squirming inside her is yours, and if you don't want me to fuck it out of her, replacing it with my own, you'll show so goddamn respect. You hold no power here."

The simmering rage bubbles within the marrow of Viktor's bones, begging to be set free, and God, I want to be here for that show.

"Okay," the cop exhales on a rugged breath. "What do you want?"

"What evidence was recovered here about Elizabeth's disappearance?"

He gets himself into a sitting position, snatching

the tissue from the hand Viktor offers to him and cleans himself off. "If you want to hide evidence, you're too late. Everything has been photographed, bagged, and tagged." He flexes his jaw, and I debate relieving him of it if he doesn't prove useful soon. "Why did you take her, you sick prick?" he spits in my direction.

Why does everyone think I took her? They have no clue how devoted to me she was—*is*. I wouldn't need to take her.

I aim his gun and fire. The sound ricochets through the room as the bullet lands with a juicy splat right in his thigh. The chorus of his cry of pain and my sister's wail of fear, mixed with Viktor's growl of annoyance, feeds the beast swimming under the skin I wear to contain it.

"We didn't take Bethany, fuckhead," I snarl. "Now, what evidence did you take from here? This is the last time I'm going to ask you. The next bullet goes in *her*."

Her gasp echoes through her sobs. I won't kill her, but a bullet to the arm never killed anyone. Or has it? No.

"Not Elizabeth. Josey." He shakes his head. "You took her. Why?"

Oh, this fucking cop doll appears to be so popular today.

"Because I'm the fucking bad guy," I sneer.

Moving toward him, I bend so I'm in his face.

"Rawwwwr," I growl, mimicking something fierce like a bear or a goddamn dragon. This is getting tedious now. I'm getting bored of these games. The constant fucking circles. They know who I am, yet they all act shocked and appalled when I do bad things. Well, fuck them.

"Who's the one holding the gun, asshole?" I question, my tone deadly. "It's my turn for questions, not yours." I tap the gun against his forehead, then move away from him.

"Did my dear friend just ask you a question?" Viktor pipes up, reminding the dumb cop he better start talking, quick.

His eyes dart between us and become glossy, the blood creating a crimson pool on the carpet beneath his leg. Slug went in deep. That's going to leave a scar. Good.

"Nothing useful," he answers, his voice sharp. "Some blood traces near the front door. A struggle took place. There was a tracking device left on the porch with a note."

"What did the note say?" I demand.

"Revenge is best served in blood. Or something to that affect," he wheezes, his lids lowering. *Stay with us, fucker.*

"To that affect or was that what it said?!"

"That's what it said," he grits out, and sways, the pain clearly making him woozy.

What the hell does that even fucking mean?

Who is she getting revenge on?

Is she using my doll to get to Viktor? But why? Maybe to turn me against him.

"Would she want payback for anything you've done?" I ask Viktor, suddenly twitchy at the thought I'm just a pawn in a bigger game.

Viktor rises to his full height. The atmosphere in the room heats, licking over us like the breath of a dragon waiting to take flight and destroy everything.

"I was loyal to Lucy and gave her more than anyone

else ever had. There is absolutely nothing she would have a quarrel with me over, so stop looking your accusing glare this way and take a look in the mirror." His tone is cold, dead. Pained.

Red and blue lights flash through the window. My paranoid thoughts took me hostage. I let the situation get beyond my control and acted erratically, shooting a weapon for all the neighbors to hear.

Viktor peeks through the curtains and curses.

"We don't have time for this," he snaps. "Let's go."

I follow him to the back entrance and stop in the doorway. "Maybe we should take her with us for leverage for after we give Dillon the cop doll," I suggest.

A cracking resounds and two officers burst through the front door, guns raised.

"Shoot!" Dillon's partner orders, and before I can get out the way, the sound of their guns discharging pops in the air like lightening. I'm moving, being dragged out of the line of fire and through the house out the back toward our car. I shoot a few rounds back at them, which makes them pause and take cover, giving us enough time to get inside the car and throttle the gas. The skidding of the rubber against asphalt sends smoke billowing—like we're in some old school movie, bank robbers on a getaway. My adrenaline kicks in and I'm vibrating with excitement. Living on the edge is thrilling, and where I should be.

"What now?" I grin over to Viktor, and my smile fades. His features are pinched. My eyes drop to the arm hugging his side. Blood blooms over his shirt.

He's been fucking hit.

No. I can't lose him.

My gut clenches at my own thoughts. A sorrow seeps through me and I suddenly realize I care more about him than I ever thought.

I'd miss him.

Fuck.

CHAPTER EIGHT

~ Severed ~

Dillon

"WHAT HAPPENED TO YOU?" Jade hisses the moment I fall into a chair in the conference room where she's camped out.

I avert my gaze from her concerned hazel eyes and stare at MJ who plays with her doll on the floor. She's trying to feed it Goldfish and making an orange, crumbly mess all over the carpet. Jade, ever the good mom, will have this room tidied up and looking better than before by the time she leaves.

"Dillon. Answer me right now."

I lift my head and meet her stare. My chest aches because I have to tell her. I have to tell her he's alive. He's real. He's still haunting us, but in the flesh.

My poor, brave girl.

She's going to freak the fuck out over this.

"Babe..." I pinch the bridge of my nose and exhale loudly.

"Stay here with daddy," Jade instructs to MJ in a faux cheery voice.

She disappears from the room without another word,

and I chance a peek at my daughter. Today, Jade's dressed her in a yellow dress that looks like it's probably annoying my little tomboy. MJ has cheesy stains all down the front and her matching yellow bow has been pulled off. Her dark, silky waves hang in her face as she talks softly to her doll.

She'll never be safe.

As long as Benny exists, my family will live in fear.

"Well, if it isn't little MJ looking too cute in her pretty dress," Edna from dispatch croons. "Aunty Edna has animal crackers for her favorite girl."

The old woman waddles over to my daughter, and MJ abandons the doll to go hug one of the grandmotherly figures in her life. I'm still staring at them when Jade hisses at me.

"Up. Now. Come on."

I groan as I stand. Jade walks with purpose and a strength only a woman who's been through what she has could ever possess. Her ass is plump and bitable now that she's big and pregnant with baby number two. I want to put a lot more babies in her, which means I need to fix this whole Benny shitstorm.

She guides me into the men's restroom where a first aid kit sits on the counter, and I lock the door behind me. The last thing I need is anyone from the department knowing about what just went down with Benny and Harris. I need to figure out a plan of action. Protocol has to take a backseat this one time.

"I can tell by the look on your face that whatever it is, it's bad. I'm ready. Just tell me." She sets to cleaning the blood from my neck as she waits.

"I just had an altercation with…him," I say on a sigh. "Benny."

She tenses and her brows furl together. "He's dead." Even though she's speaking the words of denial, she knows it deep down. I told her we had suspicion that he wasn't dead, but now we have actual visual confirmation. As if my words finally sink in, she curses. "Fuck!"

"He wants Elizabeth," I grumble.

Fat tears well in her eyes as she roughly cleans my throat. I wince, but don't tell her she's not being gentle. Her head is elsewhere at the moment.

"He can't have her," she bites out as a tear rolls down her cheek. "He can't have any of us."

I reach up and swipe away the wetness with my thumb. "He has Josey."

Her nostrils flare and she sniffles. "W-What?"

"And now he wants to bargain with her." I grit my teeth. "He'll give Josey back if we help him get Elizabeth."

"I thought he was the one you thought had Elizabeth in the first place," she cries out, dropping the soiled gauze.

I grip her jaw and plant a kiss on her trembling lips. "I'm going to fix everything. I'll get them both back and make sure that fucker dies for real this time."

"Who has her then?" she questions, steeling her voice as she goes back to unwrapping butterfly bandages.

"They think a woman named Lucy, an alias for Jessica Johnson, who worked with Harris, the owner of The Vault, who I went to bring in for questioning."

Her eyes widen at the word "they," and then again at the last part of my statement. My detective wife is smart. She can put together pieces of a puzzle quickly too.

"Benny and Harris are working together." Not a question from her soft voice, a statement. "He's been under our noses this entire time." She frowns and looks up at me. "Why hasn't he come after us?"

"Honestly, I don't fucking know. But now, he seems to have his sights set on a new obsession," I say, my head starting to fucking hurt.

"Elizabeth." She lets out a choked sob. "Oh, Dillon, what are we going to do? We can't let him take her, but he already has Josey. He's a monster. He'll hurt them."

I lean forward and kiss the flesh near her ear. "That's why I've got to figure out a plan. One the department won't trample all over with bureaucracy and red tape. This will all have to be done quickly and by our own rules."

She finishes bandaging me up and takes my cheeks in her palms. "You do whatever you have to do to end him and get those girls back." Her eyes darken. "Anything, Dillon. We can't let him destroy us again."

I twist her in my arms and face her toward the mirror as I press against her from behind. My eyes are feral. Manic almost. Hers are sad, but fierce. We're a team. We will get through this.

She reaches her hand up behind her and threads it through my hair. Our mouths meet in desperation. Through a kiss, I assure her she's mine. I won't let that motherfucker hurt her or our little girl. My hands grope her gigantic tits and I devour the sweet whimpers that pour from her mouth.

Jade needs more reassurance.

"You're mine, babe," I grunt, then nip at her lip. "This is mine." I rub at her swollen belly.

"Dillon," she whines. "I need…"

I know exactly what she needs. Benny dead. Me claiming her. Our world to be simple again. I can at least give her one of those things right now. She doesn't protest when I begin inching her dress up to her hips. Her hands fly to the edge of the seat so she can brace herself, and I push her panties down her thighs. In our next breath, I'm inside her.

Her hazel eyes meet mine in the mirror—frantic and needy and terrified—and her mouth parts. I thrust hard into my wife as I grip her tits and pull her against my chest.

"Mine," I remind her as I press kisses down the side of her face to her neck. I nip at the flesh there and revel in the way her pussy clenches when I bite her.

"Yours." She rolls her eyes back when I locate her clit. I assault her body with pleasure—from every direction. It doesn't take long for her to come hard around my cock, and I drain my own release on a ragged grumble.

I'm still situated inside her, my cock softening and releasing my seed, when she speaks again.

"I want him dead."

I kiss her earlobe. "I'm going to be the one to kill him for you."

"You've been what?" I hiss on the phone to Marcus.

"Shot. That motherfucker shot me." His voice is weak and worry niggles at me.

"Where are you?" I demand. Part of me calls to rush over to help my partner, but this is bigger than us. Lives are at stake right now. Time is of the essence.

"Broughton called an ambulance. We'll be headed to the hospital soon." He grunts in pain. "But him and that Harris fuck showed up. Scared the hell out of my girl…"

"Who?"

"Elise. Anyway, she's okay, just shaken up a bit. Any word on Josey or Elizabeth?"

Here's where I should tell my partner what happened. But I can't afford to fuck this up.

"Working on it," I grumble as I cruise through town on my mission.

"That doesn't sound reassuring whatsoever."

"I'll handle it."

He's silent for a beat, then he hisses out, "Whatever you're doing, man, be careful." His breath comes out sharp. "We need to bring those psychopaths down." In Marcus-speak: at any cost.

I get the message loud and clear.

"Keep me posted on anything you hear," I bark out as I roll into the parking lot behind an old abandoned grocery store. I hang up the phone and tuck it into my breast pocket. All my weapons are loaded and ready to go. With Benny, you can never be too sure.

I don't see any other cars and am pleased to know I got here first. That means I can stake the place out a bit before they arrive. The bandages on my neck pull at my flesh and the cut stings, but after a quick bathroom fuck with Jade, I'm feeling energized and ready to deal with these pricks.

Climbing out of the car, I do a cursory sweep, looking for anything odd or out of place. It's dark now, and all that can be heard is the wind as it whistles through the trees.

Dry leaves scrape along the pavement, giving this location an even more eerie feeling.

I keep my Glock ready in hand with a bullet chambered. If I need to pop Benny in the head for getting out of line, I won't hesitate. He's breathed Jade's air for far too long. The asshole should be grateful for every single breath he's taken the past few years. Soon, he won't get anymore.

"Ah, so the good detective can actually do something right for once in his life." Benny's voice echoes off the building, and I freeze. My eyes dart around the shadows, but I don't see him.

I grit my teeth before barking out, "Where's Josey?"

Whimpering resounds from in front of me as she staggers out from the open door of the building. Josey's hands are bound in front of her and there's a covering over her eyes. Her mouth has a strip of duct tape over the front and she's only wearing her underwear with what looks like bandages across her tits. What the fuck has he done to her?

"It's okay," I call out. "You're going home."

She starts running toward the sound of my voice, but then, as if God strikes her, she's jerked backwards and lands on her ass with a scream that's barely muffled by the tape. From behind her, Benny walks out holding one end of a rope I now realize is tied to Josey's waist.

"Bad dog," Benny chides.

"Enough with the games," I growl. "You wanted the laptop and my help in exchange for her. Was this all some ploy to get me alone?"

Benny walks over to Josey and drags her to her feet by her hair. "If I wanted to kill you, I'd have done that earlier today," he snarls. "Just like if I wanted to gut this bitch and drag her entrails around this parking lot, I would. But I need you to find Bethany." He frowns at the mention of Bethany, and the vulnerability he can't mask bleeds through, if only for a moment.

"I'm not reneging on my end of the deal. Now, give me the woman," I snap and crack my neck, my finger hovering over the trigger of my Glock.

He shoves her and she stumbles forward. I don't move to go get her in case it's a trap, but I do speak to her so she'll follow my voice. "Over here, sweetheart." Josey may have always been a pain in my ass, but now she's a victim. Just like Jade. Just like Macy. Just like my niece Jasmin. Just like Elizabeth. His reach on terrorizing women is mind boggling.

"Where's Harris?" I demand the moment I have Josey pulled against me. She sobs and trembles. "Get in the car," I murmur as I quickly untie the rope at her wrists and waist, keeping my eyes on Benny the entire time.

She yanks the covering over her eyes and rips away the tape, letting loose a cry. "They have another girl," she chokes out.

"It's okay. Just get in the car," I command again. Wisely, she scrambles into the car as if she wants to be far away from Benny. I can't say I blame her.

Benny walks over to the pole in the parking lot bearing the only light and crosses his arms over his chest. Under the yellow glow with bugs buzzing all around, he looks every bit some vicious demon recently summoned from hell. I could put a bullet right between his eyes if I wanted. Right this second. I'm tempted. I could take my own chances of finding Elizabeth.

Harris steps out of the abandoned grocery story holding a gun aimed at me. What the fuck?

"Just in case you get any ideas," he taunts. This fucker is a mind reader.

I grit my teeth. "I'm not going to go back on our deal."

He comes to stand beside Benny beneath the light as if they're a united front. But I see the distaste written all over Benny's features as he glares at me. He hates me. If I didn't have Harris's laptop and the means to help get Elizabeth back, he would be more than happy to kill me now.

"We should wrap this up and be on our way," Harris croons to Benny. And Benny actually listens to him.

He's playing Benny.

The monster of all monsters is letting some smug prick in a suit control him.

Well, that's fucking interesting.

"Where's the other woman?"

"The deal was for the cop doll. No one else," Benny spits in my direction.

"At least give me a name."

"Why?" Benny growls.

"Kami Long," Harris bellows. "I believe both her ankles are broken and her wrist. She has lacerations all over her body. Right, Benjamin?" He turns his head and cocks it slightly, as if he's not going to move another inch until Benny agrees. And to my utter damn amazement, Benny nods with a grin.

"I hope she never walks again," Benny mutters under his breath.

Harris's jaw ticks, but other than that small tell, he

seems outwardly cool. I may be able to use this woman to eliminate Benny after all. Clearly, Harris cares about her in some capacity and Benny hurt her for whatever reason. I'll find out why.

"Let me help her," I order.

Benny starts forward, but Harris grabs a fistful of his jacket. His hateful glare is turned from me to Harris.

"You don't need her anymore. Let her get some help. She'll die otherwise," Harris tries to reason.

Benny meets the psychotic man's stare without flinching. "I don't care if she dies."

"You don't need her to prove a point. You have my attention. You've always had my attention," Harris mutters softly, only for Benny's ears, though I hear. Of course I fucking hear. "Always. I think I've more than proven that."

Benny's coiled frame seems to relax. This time, his eyes ignite in resignation, and dare I say, trust.

"I'll think about it," Benny tells him.

Harris slowly walks my way. The shadows engulf him as he leaves his hellish friend behind.

"Take good care of her and you will be rewarded," Harris murmurs to me once he's near.

I bristle at his words, but this confirms my earlier suspicions. Benny hurt this woman trying to get to Harris. Why he's still working with Benny is beyond me.

He opens the back door of my car and leans in over Josey. I don't want to be caught off guard, so I back up and hold the car door open to watch him and keep my eye on Benny.

"Until we meet again, Detective," he says with a wolfish grin, slipping back out of the car. The sneaky little bastard already has his laptop in hand as he shuts the door.

Stalking away from me, he makes his way back over to Benny. They seem satisfied with the exchange, but Benny is tight with nerves. I didn't think the psycho had feelings, but apparently, he has some for his sister. And I feel like an asshole for being glad his attention on my wife seems to have disappeared altogether. I don't dare bring that shit up again.

"How will I contact you if I have information?" I ask.

Harris grins. It's positively evil. "Oh, we'll find you. We'll always find you. You can be sure of that."

If that's not a motherfucking threat, I don't know what is.

"Go do your police shit and find my doll," Benny growls.

I don't acknowledge him with an answer. I simply climb back in my vehicle and haul ass out of there.

"He slipped this in my hand," Josey whispers from the backseat as she leans forward and hands me a slip of paper.

"Did he hurt you?" I ask, though I'm not sure I want to know the answer.

"No."

Uncurling the paper, I discover directions written beneath the name Kami. I call it in and get a crew out there.

"I can take you to the hospital or we can go get this Kami woman," I say, my eyes locating Josey's in the mirror. "We're real close."

I want to get Josey out of here, but leaving that woman at the mercy of Benny goes against everything I am. They must not be going back, otherwise Harris wouldn't have given us the note with her location on it.

"No, let's go get her," Josey says, her voice adamant.

There's a keypad on the door, but Harris has already thought of that and wrote down the code. This place is a bunker. Built into the ground, I dread what I'm going to find down there and wonder how long he's had this. Furthermore, who he's kept down here. It's been three years, and I'd thought he was dead. He could have done a shitload of damage in three years.

I make Josey stay in the car so she can radio me if anyone shows up. When I reach the bottom of the stairs inside the bunker, I find myself in a kitchen of sorts. This place is lined shelf after shelf with canned goods and other end-of-the-world shit. I navigate through the small space, my Glock drawn just in case. Eventually, I pass a bedroom and find a creepy-as-fuck room that has Benny written all over it.

My gaze skims across glass-like cells that run along the back wall. Three of them. On one end, a woman lies inside on the floor, blood everywhere. She's not conscious and looks too pale. I holster my weapon and rush to disengage her door. It's locked, but after a few hard kicks, I knock it loose. Once I have the door open, I'm able to reach inside to check her pulse on her clammy neck. It's faint but there.

"Backup's arrived." Josey's voice comes through the radio, and I sag in relief. Moving the woman's hair from her face, a frown pinches my features. She's the girl from The Vault when we first went to see Harris.

"What you got?" I hear shouted down.

"We need paramedic ASAP," I bark back.

"They're here," I assure her. "You're safe now."

A flurry of activity consumes the space, and Kami is eventually stretchered to safety and taken to hospital. I send Josey with her.

"I want everything bagged and tagged," I order. "I want this place gone through with a fine-tooth comb."

"There're surveillance cameras hidden everywhere in this place," an officer announces, pulling a wire from the plaster and chasing it around the room.

"I want to know where the feed is going. Get a tech on it now."

Was this what he planned for Elizabeth?

To keep her down here in his bunker?

Not on my fucking watch.

CHAPTER NINE

~ Mutilated ~

Viktor

I PULL UP THE TRACKERS for Lucy and ignore the hostility radiating from Benny.

He really hates my affection for Kami, but instead of questioning why he feels so strongly about it, he deflects.

Giving Dillon Scott the location of the bunker was a risk, but Kami wouldn't outlast Benny's wrath and she would have died before he agreed to free her.

He'll be angry when he learns of her freedom, but unless Dillon tells him, he won't know I had anything to do with it. Josey could have traced our journey back there. It was only a short drive, and even blindfolded, she could count the time passed as it was only two right turns.

"Well?" Benjamin growls, his tone impatient.

I tap over the keys and point to the red blinking light still active on the screen. "Her car tracker is still live, but I fear it could be a trap."

"Let's go see."

His heart is now ruling his head. Walking into a trap could get us all killed. I know there is no reasoning with him when it comes to this, however.

"Can you think of any reason she would hold a grudge against you?" I enquire. None of this makes sense. Unless Lucy has simply become obsessed with the allusive monster that sits right there on the surface of who he is, things don't add up. And if there's one thing I don't enjoy, it's not knowing the reason behind someone's madness.

"She's just a cunt," Benjamin sneers.

"As much as I agree with that terminology, there has to be something driving her. She spelled out revenge. Revenge for what? Think, Monster," I demand.

He fidgets in his seat and glares at me from the corner of his eye. "I don't have enemies…well, unless you count Dillon shit-of-a-detective Scott."

"What about your dolls in the past?"

His frame solidifies and he remains silent. The air congeals and is almost unbearable. My eyes slowly drag to his and my stomach twists with the look he holds in his stare. So much damage haunting his eyes. I've never seen him look so human, so broken, so vulnerable.

"I've searched my whole life for Bethany. Only her. When my dollies were wrong, they needed to die. I lived my life alone until Jade and Macy, then my Bethany finally came home to me." He slams his fist on the steering wheel and hisses. "Lucy would never be one of them." An irritated sound leaves his throat. "This can't be about me. It can't be. This isn't my fault. She can't take her from me again. I won't survive it again. Why do people keep taking my doll from me? Why can't I just be happy, left alone with what's mine?" he mumbles in a tirade. His head bows and he pulls the car over to a stop before pushing the door open and stepping outside.

He paces, manic and panicked.

I watch in confusion, and my insides crumble when he begins screaming into the air. It's tortured and heartbreaking. The tendons in his neck bulge as he roars over and over into nothing. His whole body is rigid and straining.

Eventually, he falls to his knees, and as if summoned by his pain, thunder booms from above and heavy rain follows, pelting down around him, bouncing off the car, creating a melody to mask his grief.

Stepping from the car, I shout, "You're getting soaked. Get in the car," but he ignores me and I notice his torso softly shaking.

I stalk over to him and take a knee in front of him before pushing back on his shoulders. His head tilts up to meet mine. My heart constricts at the sight of him crying. Dark brown orbs full of tears and distress. He's a wreckage, all the emotions inside colliding and finally crashing into him all at once.

He grabs hold of me and burrows his face into my shoulder.

I can't breathe or move or fucking speak. I just hold him while he falls apart in my arms. He's screaming against my skin, agony in every ripped cry. Tears build in my own eyes, his sorrow infectious. His emotion tangible and consuming. I wrap my arms around his shoulders and hold him tight to me. I don't dare speak. I don't hold the man, or the monster. I hold the little boy who had everything taken from him. He weeps as his demons torture him, suffocating and tightening the noose. He blames himself for Bethany, not Elizabeth, the *real*

Bethany he lost so long ago.

I don't know how long we stay locked together on the side of road, but all of a sudden, Benny pushes away from me and gets to his feet. His footfalls slap the wet asphalt. When he reaches the car, he gets back inside and slams his door. I'm soaked through to my core. The rain picks up speed, hammering down on top of me. I'm stunned frozen for a few seconds, and when he honks the horn, impatient, I follow suit and slip back into the vehicle. We're both dripping and shivering. Benny doesn't even wait until my door is fully closed before he takes off, fishtailing on the soaked pavement. After ten minutes of driving in silence, we pull up to my home.

"We should change, then check out the tracker," he announces.

We both know Lucy isn't going to be with the car. If she cut out her neck tracker, she will know the car is also bugged. But wherever she's left it will be deliberate, a message or clue.

Benny exits the car and strips through the house all the way to the shower. The bathroom door slams in my face as I follow behind him. He's angry at himself for showing emotion. I pull out some clothes for both of us and wait. My clothes begin to itch, chilling me to the bone. Stripping them off, I stand there bare as the bathroom opens and Benny appears within the frame, steam billowing behind him like he just stepped from hell itself.

A towel sits on his hips and his chest rises and falls in fast pants. His muscles pull taut and water rivulets slide down over the ridges. He's still in a state of heightened emotion—something he's not used to dealing with.

"It's okay," I say as I walk over to him. When I reach up to touch his face, he backs away, a glare on his face. "It's okay," I repeat.

I doubt he's ever showed emotion like that to another living being, and in his eyes, it's a weakness. He will be fighting with the beast inside to stop from killing me just to prove to me—to him—he's still the monster and the master. I know that because it's what would be happening inside me.

His entire torso ripples with energy and I almost expect him to lash out and hit me—to beat me until I'm quivering and begging the monster for mercy.

I'll take it if that's what he needs to gain control again. If that's what he needs to feel whole.

"It's not a weakness to feel," I placate.

His eyes flare and he sneers. "You think I'm weak now?"

"No," I reply, quick and reassuring, but my voice sounds soft to my own ears. Like I'm comforting a child.

"You think I'm some pussy bitch now because I allowed you to see that side of me?" he growls.

"No," I repeat firmer, squaring my shoulders as he advances toward me.

"You think I'm going to let you be my puppet master? My sugar daddy now?"

His temper is almost palpable. He's stunning in his rage. Power. Aggression. My dick thickens at the sight of him, and his eyes drop to where I'm naked to his scrutiny. He smirks, cruel and mocking. "You want me to be your bitch now? Let you fuck my ass because you saw me cry. You *forced* me to feel," he screams. "You fucking kept prying and prying, like it's my fault Bethany is gone."

"No, that's untrue. I care about you and want to get her back, so I need to know why she was taken."

"You don't care why. You're glad she's gone so you can have me to yourself, so you can try to make me *your* doll." His eyes are wild, his pupils expanding rapidly like he's on a high he can't control.

"You know that's not true. I want to find her. For you."

"Liar," he roars, almost chest to chest with me now, his skin giving off a heat, beckoning for me to taste him.

"You want me, don't you?" he taunts.

"Stop it," I warn.

"You want me for yourself."

"Stop it."

"You think you can take me, *Viktor*?"

I push at his shoulders, causing him to stumble back. It's slight and he's back in control of his body within seconds.

"You lie to yourself and ignore your attraction to me," I goad, meeting him glare for glare. I shove him again. "You want me to take you. To fuck you. To own you," I tease, making him almost combust with rage.

"I'd never let you *take* me or fucking *own* me," he booms. "*I'm* the master here. You're *my* doll!" he screams louder, almost shattering the glass of the windows.

Ripping his towel from his waist, he throws it to the ground, his thick cock bouncing. Hard. Jerky. Needy. With a roar of rage, he shoves me back onto the bed. Then, with the power of a beast, he flips me onto my stomach and growls, "No one owns me. I'm the fucking master here. *I'm* the master. I'm the fucking master. I own *you*."

CHAPTER TEN

~ Smashed ~

Dillon

The monitor is making my eyes blur. I'm tired and hungry. My eyes dart to the office where I've set up a bed for MJ.

"She's okay," Jade assures me. "It's like an adventure for her. She's surrounded by family."

I can't stand the fact that my daughter is held up in the precinct because I can't risk Benny having any chance of turning on us and taking my girls.

"I hate this. I don't want my daughter to have to look over her shoulder her whole life. What happens if we don't get Beth back alive?" I breathe my fear into the room and Jade rubs my shoulders.

"You will. You'll find her and kill him."

Damn, I hope she's right. This job has taken its toll on me. I feel old. I feel fucking defeated.

"Maryann's flight gets in tonight. We should collect her from the airport. She's been through so much already. She shouldn't have to still be dealing with Stanton's fuck-ups," Jade murmurs.

I grunt. "We shouldn't still be having to deal with

Stanton's fuck-ups either, yet here we are. Just sitting and waiting for the next blow." I can't take much more of this. Every single day this job takes a chink out of my soul.

"Here," Jacob announces, tapping at the screen. "I found where it leads back to and downloaded everything it's recorded since it was set up."

Harris's IP address. Of course it was his setup. "Are you going to release me now?"

I signal for Reeves to take Jacob back to the holding room.

"You promised you would drop me home after I helped," he grinds out.

"And I will," I bite back, "but I may need you again and I'm not searching for you if I do. So, until I know for sure, you can stay where I can locate you. Reeves will go bring you some snacks."

Jacob is a hacker too clever for prison. The moment this shit started going down with Harris, I had them pull him and bring him to the station so we could strike a deal. He's an asset to this precinct because he has a valuable skillset. And the moment this case is closed, he can go on his merry little way as we bargained.

Jade moves around me, taking the seat Jacob just vacated. "Let me watch through this. You said you had a name to look into."

Right. Lucy. Real name Jessica Johnson. I search her name in the database and the internet. It's surprising how much information we find simply by using Google or Facebook. An article about a couple, Fred and Marla Johnson, dying in a boating accident comes up. They were survived by one daughter, Jessica Johnson.

A missing person's report pings in our database, listed with the runaways.

"If she was the only child and they were wealthy enough to own that boat," Jade says as she raps her finger on my screen, "then they must have left money."

"You're supposed to be watching that feed history, not worrying about what I'm doing," I tease.

"It's boring so far," she huffs. "Nothing of interest at all."

I look into the Johnson's wealth, and Jade's right. They left money and property. "They owned a small chain of motels," I grumble at her being right. Everything was left to their daughter. "If she's a runaway, she wouldn't have claimed her inheritance."

"Or the system wasn't updated for when she came of age. She's not a child runaway after she's reaches eighteen," Jade points out. "Oh, here we go."

Jade hisses, looking back at her screen.

Benny appears on the monitor and Jade clutches my hand, squeezing so tight, the blood stops pumping to my fingers and they turn numb. "I can watch from here," I tell her, rubbing her back.

"No, it's fine."

He's not alone. Elizabeth is with him. I don't need to see this. I want to look away, but it's like a train wreck you can't help but stare right at it.

Moments pass in silence and Jade almost relaxes in the chair. "He's so different with her." She sighs, relief evident in her tone.

"What do you mean?"

She tilts her head, studying the screen. "Like he cares

what she thinks and how she feels."

"And?" I growl.

"He wasn't like that with me. It was about what he needed and punishing me. Domination. With her, he's not punishing. More like worshipping her. And she's not fighting," she says, astonished. "She's completely compliant."

"She's brainwashed," I grunt.

"Or she's just as messed up as him. Benny, Chief, now Beth. It's in their blood. The crazy runs through their veins, polluting their minds."

"Do you really believe that?" a small, strained voice questions from behind us, startling us both.

"Elise," Jade stammers, jumping to her feet.

"You really think crazy runs in our veins?" she asks.

"No, not yours," Jade assures her. "I didn't mean…"

"What about our children?" Tears well in Elise's eyes as she clutches her stomach.

What the fuck?

"No, she didn't mean that. What are you doing here?" I ask, concerned.

"Marcus wanted me to come here and stay with Jade and MJ until he's discharged." She moves closer. "What are you watching?" she asks, and her mouth parts upon seeing the screen with her two siblings.

Jade quickly turns and clicks to the next activity. Benny is there with that woman Kami. He's beating her.

"Oh my God," Elise cries out.

Jade tries to stop the video, but instead hits the volume, and Kami's screams ring out into the silent precinct. "Stop, stop." Jade panics, and I rush to help her, exiting the entire program. Jade is panting, her distress evident in her eyes. Seeing Benny hurting Kami brings with it memories of her time with him. Witnessing his brutality on others. "Dillon," she breathes, her eyes growing so large, they almost eclipse her forehead. She's holding her stomach.

"What is it?" I ask, fearing for both her and our baby.

My heart pounds erratically in my chest.

"My water just broke," she gasps.

Oh, fuck.

"It's too early." Her bottom lip trembles.

Fuck. Fuck.

"It will be okay," I assure her. "The baby is big enough. People have them early all the time."

She nods in agreement as I scoop her up. Her dress is soaked and the floor is a small puddle. My heart almost stops when I see blood mixed with the clear fluid. "Elise, stay with MJ."

"Of course."

Pacing the hospital corridor is familiar to me. I fucking hate this place. Marcus sits in his wheelchair twiddling his thumbs, and watching him is making me more nervous. He came down to help calm me and it's having the opposite effect. He's fucking nervous and it's ramping up my own anxiety.

"Mr. Scott?" a doctor calls out, and I almost tackle him.

"Yes, that's me."

His eyes drop to Marcus, who's wheeled almost over

the doctor's toes. "It's fine. He can hear what you have to say. Just tell me."

"There was some internal bleeding and we had to deliver the child via an emergency cesarean section. Your baby is in the NICU receiving oxygen and being monitored. He will need shots to help his lungs finish developing, but it looks positive."

"He?" I choke out. A boy.

"Yes. Congratulations."

"And Jade?" Marcus demands.

"The mother is still heavily sedated, but we expect her to make a full recovery."

"Oh, thank God," I sigh, bringing the reluctant doctor in for a hug. "Can I see her?" I beg as I release him.

"She's being moved to recovery. When she's ready, I'll send the nurse for you."

"Thank you," I utter. "Thank you."

He nods and retreats.

"Congrats." Marcus grins up at me. "A son."

"Yeah, a son."

"Elise is pregnant," Marcus announces, and my smile falls.

"I got that impression." I stare down at him. If anything, this scare with our child and Jade has taught me that life is unpredictable and too short for us to deny love. "If you love her, then you should make a go of things," I tell him.

He blanches. Shocked. "She lied to me."

"Sometimes we all lie to get what we want."

"You're not mad?"

"Oh, I am mad, but I'll get over it, and hell…" I tease

as I kick his foot. He flinches. "She could do a lot worse."

I mean, after all, her sister hooked up with Benny the psycho of all people. Marcus is one of the good guys.

"Fuck."

Yeah. Fuck.

CHAPTER ELEVEN

~ *Disintegrated* ~

Benny

Mine. Mine. Mine.
   The chanting in my head won't stop.

Rage has clouded my vision and I've transformed into the beast I can barely contain. The monster.

"Benjamin."

His voice. Calm. Soothing. Comforting. It parts through the red haze and finds me. Splashes cold water on my blazing soul. Reminds me I'm not alone.

But he betrayed you.

Did he, though?

He's here, bent over his bed, in complete submission. Master bows for one. He bows for me. My hand trembles and I fist it. The urge to strike him over and over again is overwhelming. His powerful back decorated in beautiful tattoos screams of stories I haven't been told. Stories I'm desperate to hear.

Why?

Why do I care so fucking much?

"Benjamin," he says, "we're a team."

A team.

The thought is still foreign, even after all this time.

I drop my fisted hand to the middle of his spine, but I don't hit him. Instead, I find my palm splaying out to touch the tattooed flesh.

"Benjamin. We're a *family*. You. Me. Bethany."

Now, his words find their intended mark. My heart hammers in my chest. I always wanted a brother. Would this have been what it was like? Someone always looking out for you? Someone who seemingly loved you no matter what sort of fucked up shit you did?

"He took them away. He took my family away." I blink and growl and slap the side of my head to drive away thoughts of my father. The way he destroyed everything—everyone I loved. How he fucked with my head over and over again.

"Benjamin." The voice is hard. Firm. Demanding.

I open my eyes to find him farther up the bed, lying on his back with his arms outstretched like Christ on the cross. Like he's offering himself to me. A sacrifice to the beast.

I prowl up the bed, my feral instincts taking over. I'm intrigued as fuck over the use of the word family. Viktor's powerful body could take mine in a second if he truly tried, but he doesn't. His cock, heavy and aroused, bobs against his lower abdomen. Each breath he takes is measured and controlled.

Straddling his muscular thighs that bear nearly as much hair as mine, I find myself fascinated at the fact my dick is erect as well. I want to inhale him and see if he smells like family. I want to taste him to see if he tastes like family.

His dark eyes lock with mine as I lean forward. My dick rubs against his and a choked sound escapes me. I hate the desperate quality of it. Shame ripples through me, hurtling me back to the past with my psycho fucking parents, but it's Viktor—my brother of sorts—who brings me back to him.

"Benjamin."

That's all he says. My name. Just like Bethany would say it. The old her. The new her. Loving. Caring. Fucking sweet.

"You're my doll," I snarl. "I *made* you."

He smirks and slightly thrusts his hips at me. His dick rubs against mine again, sending pleasure sparking down my spine. "We belong together, yes."

"She's my *doll*," I challenge. I don't understand this. I don't understand the dynamics or my fucking brain. How I want two different things.

"A family can be made up of more than two people," he says back. "Where I come from…" he trails off, his features darkening. "Family is everything. It's the most important thing. You have your brother's back until the end."

A low growl rumbles in my throat and I snap my eyes closed. My body seems to move on its own accord. I sink down against Viktor's hard chest and seek out his heartbeat with my ear pressed to his flesh.

Thump! Thump! Thump!

He's calm. He's quiet. He's in control.

Yet his heart rages wildly in cadence with mine. When I thrust my hips against him, we both groan. Our dicks are sandwiched between us and the friction is dizzying.

"We're going to get the rest of our family back. You

must trust me, Benjamin. Always," he states, his palm clutching the back of my neck. Possessive. Owning. Greedy. "You can't always be in control. It's exhausting. This is why we need each other. When one is weak, the other can be strong."

"I'm not weak," I snap, but it's a fucking lie.

Here I am rubbing my dick against my best friend while my Bethany is out there in the hands of some sick bitch. I don't know what to fucking do about it. Until I have more information, I can't.

"You belong to me," he says simply. "And I belong to you. We'll get back your missing doll. Then, we can go back to being happy."

Happy?

It's such a foreign concept, but the past three years with Viktor have been the closest, for sure. He's given me friendship and brotherhood. Unspoken love. Different than what I feel for Bethany, but somehow just as deep.

"I don't understand it," I growl.

"You don't have to," he murmurs. "You just have to go with it."

His fingertips run along my buzzed scalp, and I groan. I want to fuck. Fuck and claim and own. Turning my face toward his chest, I scrape my teeth along his skin. The hiss coming from him makes my dick thump against his thigh. Angrily, I nip at his abs and pecs. Not hard enough to break the skin, just hard enough to warn him.

If you're fucking playing me, I'll tear you apart with my teeth.

"Get out of your head, Benjamin, and do what we

both know needs to happen. What *will* happen. What will bind us as not just friends and partners but *family*."

His words scream to my black, bloodied, motherfucking broken soul.

You're mine.

I'm yours.

We'll get her back.

I attack him as though I can steal the words from his mouth. I sure as hell try. I bite at his bottom lip, challenging him to say more. But he only grunts and angles his head to kiss me. It's not some bullshit gay fairy kiss either.

He's stealing my soul.

The motherfucker *is* the devil.

I spear my tongue into his hot mouth and show him even the devil answers to someone. My mouth possesses his as our bodies grind against one another. He's as strong as me, so when he begins manipulating our bodies in a certain way, I can't even fight it. His grip on my hips is painful—bruising even—but it makes my cock seep with need. And then his large hand is wrapped around my throbbing cock, our mouths never missing a beat on dueling with one another.

"Get your dick wet, Benjamin," he orders against my mouth.

I jerk away from him, my chest heaving with breaths, and glare. With an evil smile, I stick my fingers into his mouth, forcing them down the back of his throat, and fuck it until his eyes burn bright red and he gags. Then, I reach between us and wet my dick.

"Make this real," he urges, wild fire raging in his eyes. The mask of control has slipped and he's beastly like me in this moment. There are no masters. Only monsters. Brothers.

I've never fucked a guy. I never even considered it. Yet, Viktor doesn't even register as a sexual preference. He's just Viktor. The suited savior who's had my back since I crawled out of my burning home, barely alive.

"Fuck!" I scream. My spittle sprays his face, but he doesn't even blink. He bares his teeth at me in challenge. The vein in his throat bulges and throbs.

"Make. This. Fucking. Real."

With my eyes pinning his, I grip my cock and begin pushing the tip against his hairy ass. He's spread his thighs apart so he can accept me. At first, I meet resistance against the puckered entrance, but then, with a little power, I'm able to drive all the way in.

I want to watch him. See his face contort into one of pain. But my fucking God it feels so goddamn intense, my eyes slam shut. My balls seize up as if I'm going to blow my load right away. Instead of coming like a teenage loser, I grit my teeth and snap my eyes back open.

His eyes are swimming with lust and fire and a mutual rage. Emotions he's kept well-hidden not only swim to the surface, but they thrash there. They make themselves known. I own him. I've always fucking owned him.

He grips my throat and jerks me to him. My dick slides deeper inside him, causing us both to moan. The greedy bastard sucks my tongue into his mouth as he squeezes the shit out of my neck. Grabbing his free wrist, I pin it to the bed and begin thrusting into him without apology. I don't know if it hurts, and I don't fucking care. I just want him to know I'm the motherfucker in charge here. He's always wanted to be in charge—to be the autocratic ruler over me—but you can't master something you didn't create. You certainly can't dominate that which you crave to submit to.

Stars dance in my vision the tighter he chokes me. I thunder into him harder, as if I'll be able to split him open and replace all the parts of him with me. Our teeth nip at each other's mouths.

Two monsters dead set on ruling the other.

"Fuck," I hiss, my orgasm drawing close again.

"Make me come, Benjamin," he orders, his voice raspy and full of need.

I bite his lip hard enough that I taste blood, but find myself obeying. Releasing his wrist, I slip my hand between us and grip his cock. It's hot and thick in my hand. I stroke him like I like to be stroked—hard and furious—until he's coming with a guttural groan. The pure, animalistic sound sends me over the edge. My nuts seize up and my seed explodes from me.

Hot. Violent. Intense.

I fill him. I fucking mark him.

He rubs at his cum on his belly before making a V over my heart.

The fucker marks me too.

When our eyes meet again, I finally understand.

We're not two monsters dead set on ruling each other.

We're going to rule together.

"You sure this is the place?" I ask, my fingers thrumming against the steering wheel to a beat that only exists in my head. It's a place I've gone to before many times to buy toiletries and other items when I was younger, and then when I had my dolls, Jade and Macy. Something niggles at me. Maybe Lucy does have something against me.

Viktor, now showered and dressed in one of his damn power suits, looks at his phone app and nods. "It leads here. An abandoned drugstore. Why here, though?"

The air is charged between us, but it's no longer something foreign and strange. It's powerful. Energy only created by two people like us. Viktor was right. We're better when we operate as one. When we *become* one. My dick lurches in my jeans at the reminder, but I ignore it for now. I'm buzzing with a high I don't understand—a high Viktor injected me with. And soon, I'll have Bethany back to complete our family. I'll have both my dolls and I'll be fucking happy like Viktor claims.

Just have to clean house a bit first.

Get rid of this dumb psycho cunt.

"There," Viktor says as he points through the windshield. "See her?"

Lucy walks out from behind the dumpster in one of her stupid skintight latex black cat suits she used to wear at The Vault. Her blonde hair hangs in silky waves in front of her tits, which are all but falling out of the material. She's painted her lips bright crimson—the color of blood—and she better fucking hope it's lipstick and not my doll's blood. One of her knives is gripped tightly in her right hand and her cell is in her left. Shit is getting more twilight zone than reality. I bite the inside of my cheek to make sure I haven't slipped into some kind of coma and I'm making all of this up inside my head. She looks like something out of a bad villain movie. A chuckle almost threatens, but my rage douses the humor, and I'm back to wanting to just cut her limb from limb so I can see all the red inside her.

"I could break her neck before she could get one stab," I growl.

Viktor reaches over and squeezes my thigh. One simple touch and my head is spinning with questions. What are we now? What am I? Is this normal to bond in such a way that it goes beyond titles and gender? Beyond love and hate? Beyond what's expected even of ourselves? "Let's hear what she has to say first. Bethany could be in trouble."

Viktor. Always thinking three steps ahead.

"Right," I grunt in agreement.

He pats my jean-clad thigh and climbs out of the vehicle. I get out and follow close behind him, watching her over his shoulder.

"Evening, boys," Lucy chirps, her grin wicked. As if we're meeting up for fucking drinks. As if she doesn't have my entire world in her clutches.

Viktor makes a sound of disappointment at her, and it reminds me she doesn't have my *entire* world. Just a very important piece. "Enough with the bullshit, *Jessica*."

I smirk when her face sours at the mention of her real name.

"It's Lucy now," she spits out.

Viktor shrugs. "We all have our aliases, but you're still Jessica Johnson according to the state of Arkansas. Isn't that correct?"

"Whatever. I'm not playing your games," she snaps at him. "I knew you would follow my tracker."

Viktor glances over his shoulder at me before looking back at her. "Luring us here through your tracker is indeed a game, whether you want to admit it or not." He crosses his arms over his chest. "And I'm really good at games."

Her features pinch together angrily. "Enough! I don't care to talk. I care to trade."

This piques my interest. "What do you want?" I growl.

She laughs, throaty and loud. "Oh, you still really don't get it."

Viktor stiffens. It's definitely about me, then. I'm drawing blanks, though. Was she related to one of the dolls I'd taken? She doesn't resemble any of them. I remember their faces perfectly. Every last broken one of them.

"I want Benny." She points her knife in the air at me. Our eyes meet and she bats her lashes at me. "I want *you*."

Doesn't everyone, bitch?

"Why?" Viktor asks. "What's so special to *you* about Benjamin?" His tone is possessive and protective. It makes my chest tighten in response.

Brothers look out for each other.

Mine is standing in front of me, facing off with this psycho bitch, because he thinks he's protecting me.

Trust.

I could bypass him and slit her throat, but he wants me to trust him. Hell, I want to trust him. So, for now, I do. I remain behind him. Waiting for his cue.

"You seriously don't remember me?" she demands, her voice shrill. "What a fucking asshole! You were one then, and you're still one." Her voice cracks. "Think, Benjamin. Does this place not seem familiar to you? How about the Ace Roller Shack? Ring any bells?"

This place was just a fucking store, bitch. One I'd come to for supplies when my cunt father left us. Ace Roller Shack was a hangout for inferior snot-nosed brats.

The name unclicks something inside my brain, though.

Wait.

I study her face, wash it clean in my mind, taking the years off. The blonde hair. Jessica, Jessica, Jess, Jess. *"Jess, come on."* An irritating voice chimes in my mind. I do remember her. My thoughts expand and I'm thrust into the past.

⟶

People irritate me. Even walking past me. If their body comes too close, their mundane existence touching me, it drives me crazy. I keep my distance and don't make eye contact with the two girls giggling to each other while they keep looking over at me. All I can think about is painting their faces in the correct manner instead of the appalling attempt they've made. One looks like she has slugs for eyebrows.

Does she think that's beautiful?

"Tell her to go on the pill," the blonde of the two chirps over at me.

I turn my head in her direction, visions of scrubbing her face and body until she bleeds and her skin renews play like a vivid dream in the aisle.

"Oh God, he's just staring at you. Maybe he doesn't have a girlfriend," the redhead says before chuckling.

"He's buying condoms," the blonde argues.

The redhead shrugs her shoulders. "So?"

"I'm on the pill," the blonde blurts out, ignoring her

friend. "*Saves using those nasty things.*" *She bites her lip, and I'm hoping her teeth pierce the skin.*

They don't.

She walks toward me, and the hair on my neck prickles. She stinks of cheap perfume and she's in my space. My body stiffens as she leans up and whispers, "Come by the Ace Roller Shack sometime."

Her hair sags under the weight of the hair spray she used to keep curls in. The waves of anxiety flood through my body. Urges, strong and unthinkable, surge through my veins. I want to wash her clean in her own river of tears and blood.

"Jess, come on," the redhead complains. "He's freaking me out." Her tone is gentle, but the mocking spirals through it.

Backing away from me, they leave the aisle, and all I want to do is get the hell out of here.

"Because I turned you down?" I ask, my tone incredulous as the memory fades. I'm surprised I could recall it at all. It's only because of the events that took place after that it's even there to begin with. What a petty, irritating, worthless vendetta. "All this because I didn't go fucking roller skating with you?" This is stupid. "Petty-ass bitch."

She screeches and advances a step. Viktor snaps at her. "Stay right there."

"Yeah, *Jess*, stay right there," I mock. "I knew I should have bloodied your ugly face up in the condom aisle that day."

"Benjamin," Viktor warns.

But I'm more than pissed now. I'm not going to sit back and let this psycho cunt try to ruin my life over something so damn stupid.

"You should have!" she screams at me, fat tears welling in her eyes. "You should have done your worst right here behind this drugstore. It would have been better than what *he* did to me."

The way she says *he* has my hackles rising.

"Who?" Viktor says softly. "What did *he* do to you?"

She lets out a choked sob, then sucks her emotions down inside with a deep breath before sneering. "He followed me. After I walked my friend home, he followed me. When he flashed his red and blue lights behind me, I stopped to talk to the officer." Her body trembles, but it's unclear whether it's fear or rage. "He said there was a predator on the loose—that I should go with him. That he'd take me home." A tear rolls down her cheek, but she's quick to swipe it away. "For some stupid reason, my mind went to you. The fucking weirdo from the drugstore." Another pained sob. "I thought he was saving me from *you*."

Ha! Stupid, pathetic, mundane cunt. No one can save *you* from *me*.

I grit my teeth. "I wouldn't touch you then, and I certainly won't touch you now." A growl rumbles through me. "But I'd like to hack away at your face. It's always been a dream of mine."

"Enough," Viktor barks.

She unzips the front of her cat suit all the way to her pussy, and I stare, unimpressed when she reveals her stomach and breasts. Words are carved in scars all over her flesh. The word cunt makes me smile.

"Boo fucking hoo. Join the list of all the people my psychotic daddy tortured," I snarl. "I don't fucking care that you have scars from him. Don't we all? Bethany has nothing to do with this. Where is she?"

"Oh," she screeches. "Your sick fuck daddy didn't write these. No, these are the words he chanted while violating me. The words he called *you*."

My tendons pull taut and every urge inside me tells me to punch her jaw off her face to stop her mouth from moving.

"He had so much to say about his disappointment of a son." Her tone is dripping with hate. "He hated you and took all that hate and sank it into me."

"Who the fuck cares, whore?" I snap, hoping to end her stupid story time. "Where is Bethany?"

She points the knife out toward me. "She's fucking dead, you delusional fuck."

The breath from my lungs expires and I think I'm going to pass out.

No.

No.

No.

She's lying.

"But *Elizabeth* is alive, for now."

Thud. Thud. Thud.

The bitch *is* playing fucking games.

"Stop with the games already, you're not very good at them," Viktor warns, and I'm left sucking in air to fill my lungs.

"I'm sorry you had to be involved in this," she says to

Viktor, actual sadness in her voice. "But you chose *him* the moment he turned up at The Vault. I saw it. The enigma. The instant connection. I knew I lost you to him."

She tosses the phone at him, and he catches it easily.

"You never had me. I helped you because I could use you. Nothing more. And you made a mistake by betraying me. How ever this plays out, you will live to regret it," Viktor tells her before looking down at the screen.

A hiss escapes him that has me jerking the phone from his grip. What I see sucks the breath right from my chest. A video. Live feed, perhaps. Bethany is naked, face down in the bathtub, her blood smeared all over the white fiberglass with her wrists bound behind her at her ass. Her knees are bent and her tied ankles are attached by rope to her wrists. Water sits in the bottom half of the tub and her neck is tilted back as she desperately tries to keep her head above it. Every so often, she sucks in a deep breath, then her face falls below the surface. Towels have been rolled and stuffed on either side of her between the tub and her body so she can't move in any direction.

My heart rate skyrockets. "Where is she?" I bellow.

"Not so fast, asshole," she snaps. "If you want the girl unharmed, then you have to come with me." She points at me again with her knife as she zips up her suit. "I've been waiting for this moment my entire life. Since the moment your father made me his plaything. He told me he was watching you. Fucking following you. And then I happened to step out of that store and gain his interest. It's all your fault!"

"Tell me where the girl is," Viktor urges. "She'll drown if we don't get to her."

"You don't care about her. You're in love with him," she cackles, her red lipstick staining her top teeth. "But does he love you? That is the question. How loyal is your monster? Did you make the right choice?"

She pulls something from her back pocket. "Benny, you have a choice. You can leave with the location and go rescue your dolly. But if you choose that, I'll kill your master, and I will kill him slowly."

Images barrage into the forefront of my mind, him suffering at her hand. Dying while knowing it's my fault, but not by my hand. No. I can't lose him. I can't lose either of them. Why can't I just have my dolls and be left alone by crazy, jealous fucks wanting to cut them free of their strings? They like their strings. They love their creator, their master, their fucking monster.

"Tick tock," she spits, moving the point of her blade in Viktor's direction.

Pain at the thought of losing Viktor stings too harsh. The loss would haunt and break me. I'm too attached.

He's mine.

Mine.

Mine.

And she can't have either of them.

"What's the other option?" I growl.

"Or, you take this." She wiggles a pill at me, but looks at him. "Then, I give him the location to find your doll and you have to trust that he will look for her. But *I get you*. That's how this goes down," she says to both Viktor and me.

I glance back down at Bethany on the screen. She won't last another twenty minutes. She'll tire out and eventually drown. I grip Viktor's shoulder and squeeze.

"I need you to find her," I whisper. "I *trust* that you will."

His amber eyes widen and flicker as though flames are igniting within him. He jerks his head back over to her. "No," Viktor yells, his cool demeanor officially gone. "He's not going with you. I'll go."

She laughs. "Decisions, decisions. I can wait you out. She'll drown. I'll cut you both to shreds before the night's over anyway. I have nothing to lose."

"I'm staying," I snarl, then mutter to Viktor, "I need *you* to trust *me* too. Please find her. Take care of her."

I'll kill this bitch, I tell him with a hard gaze. *I'll make her fucking suffer.*

When she tosses me the pill, I catch it and swallow it dry. Viktor grits his teeth, but gives me a clipped nod. Time is of the essence.

"Location. Now," I bark at her.

"Get in the car first," she orders. "I don't want to have to lug your big ass any more than I have to."

I stride over to her car and she makes a point of pulling the tracker from under the hood and tossing it to the ground. She slips into the seat next to me. My limbs are heavy and I can't lift my arm to throttle her.

"Crystalline Hotel on highway fourteen. Room twenty-six. Key is under the door mat," she says coolly out the window to Viktor. "Better hurry. That's at least a fifteen-minute drive from here. Do you think she even has fifteen minutes left on her pathetic life?"

Viktor shoots me one more determined look before stalking away. The sound of the tires squealing is music to my ears.

My eyelids begin to feel heavy, and I sway from side to side in the seat.

"Now, now, sleepy," she purrs. "Not bedtime yet. We have a little change of plans. Come on. You'll be out soon, so we need to make this quick."

I'm confused when she gets back out of the car. What the fuck is she doing? Everything spins around me. She comes around to help me and I lean on her for leverage. My mind is woozy and the world becomes distorted around me.

I stumble as she leads me around the side of the building where another car is parked. She opens the backseat and I fall inside. My plans to break her neck while we drive fizzle away as blackness closes in around me. The car door slams, and then we're gone.

I fade away, hoping Viktor saves my doll.

But I don't worry about him saving me.

I'll fucking save myself.

Blink.

Blink.

Blink.

Black.

CHAPTER TWELVE

~ *Shredded* ~

Viktor

Leaving him with that psychotic bitch is the hardest thing I've ever had to do.

My hands clench the steering wheel so tight, they almost become one in the same. The GPS tells me I'm still five minutes away. Honking the horn at the traffic in front of me isn't helping keep me calm. I need to focus. Cool my blood and clear my mind.

A chaotic mind is a dangerous mind, moy brat.

My brother knew what he was talking about and each lesson he taught me has come to fruition in some form or another. I check the clock for the thousandth time and pull out into oncoming traffic, running the red light and pulling back into my own lane. Horns sound out around me, but this is life and death, so everyone else can fuck off.

I take the final right and pull into a rundown motel. The lights are out and the courtyard is overgrown with weeds. Windows are smashed and graffiti covers the walls and doors. What the hell would Jessica—Lucy never suited her anyway—be doing here? I shut the car off as soon as I get it in park and bolt from the vehicle. My feet pick up into a run as I realize I'm at the bottom end and need to be up top to number 26. Within seconds, I'm at the location.

I kick the door open, not bothering with a key, and it gives easily, practically disintegrating on impact. "Elizabeth?" I call out, scanning the room and locating the bathroom. Her body is still and her head is completely submerged in pink water. I drop to my knees and jerk her from the water by her hair, wincing at the temperature of her icy skin. That stupid bitch let cold water trickle around her, freezing Elizabeth before drowning her.

I pull her into my arms, soaking my suit, and push the wet strands of hair from her face. Quickly, I carry her over to an old beat up bed and sit with her in my lap. Since she's bound and I don't have time to untie her, I cradle her across my thighs and check her pulse, but there isn't one.

Fuck. How long was she under?

Tipping her chin, I squeeze her nose and blow into her mouth. One. Two. Stopping and placing one palm down on top of my dominant hand, I begin compressions. Back and forth, I switch from trying to pump her heart and blowing air into her lungs. Her body jerks, and as I'm blowing into her mouth for the fourth time, water rushes from her mouth into mine, forcing me away so she can cough and sputter.

"It's okay," I assure her, my tone calm.

I help tilt her to the side. Her hands and feet are still bound behind her, contorting her body at an unusual angle. Sounds of her gasps are music to my ears.

"Thank you," she rasps out, her lips a dark shade of blue. "Thank you."

I slip my jacket off and lay it over her bare form before

untying her and helping her sit beside me on the bed. She slips on my jacket and wraps it tight to her body. Fresh, weeping blood blossoms on her chest from me upsetting the healing.

"Where is he?" she asks, searching behind me.

I don't want to answer her. I feel almost at fault, like I failed him. I vetted Lucy. I had no idea about any attack on her. It makes sense, though. After getting abused by Benny's dad, she became unstable with her home life and ran away.

But why harbor such animosity for so long?

People try to tell me fate doesn't exist—that we control our own paths, but how can it be that both Jessica and Benjamin came to me and both had a connection to each other, setting off a chain of misfortunate events?

My cell phone vibrates against my leg and I use it as an excuse not to answer her straight away. I hold up my hand, signaling I need to take the call, and walk outside.

"What is it?" I bark down the line, assuming it's someone from the club. The club seems so insignificant now. My father would be so disappointed in me for letting it go down the way it has. But disappointing him is something I'm accustomed to.

"Harris," a voice growls. "It's Detective Scott."

Well, a bit too late, asshole. No wonder Benjamin detests him so much. He is useless.

"Yes?"

"I had some personal things come up, but I wanted to let you know I got the girl out."

My heart hammers in my chest and fury, untamed and ruthless, surges through me. He's lying. He's saying he has Elizabeth, to what end? To lure Benjamin in?

"Harris, are you still there? The signal's not very good at the hospital."

"Why are you at the hospital?"

"That's where I brought that Kami girl. She's in bad shape, but she's tough—a fighter. Who is she to you?"

Kami. Kami. Kami.

I'd forgotten about her.

I slipped the address for the bunker into that cop girl's hand, but then I didn't even think about her, not once afterwards. I didn't know if Dillon would go there to save Kami or not. He might have thought it was a trap and not gone after her, then she would have bled out down there in a small glass box. Bleeding out and dying while Benjamin and I—well, me at least—were satisfying a craving since the day we met. The day he called for assistance. The day he needed me. While she was potentially dying, my Benjamin, my monster, was losing himself inside me.

What does all this even mean?

One thing's for certain: shit has changed irrevocably.

My eyes draw up to see Elizabeth has moved to the door and is watching me. Some color has sprung to her cheeks and her lips don't seem as blue.

"She's just an employee," I lie.

"Well, I'd say it was more than that, but she will tell me soon enough," Dillon grumbles. He sounds how I feel. Worn out.

I didn't even calculate the risk of letting Dillon take Kami. She's loyal, but damn, she's angry. I also thought Lucy—er—Jessica would never betray me, and she did. Kami knows too much about me. Who I really am. I can't risk leaving her where he can interrogate her.

Dillon clears his throat, and I want to reach through the phone and rip it out so he can't ask her anything.

"Anyway, I did some digging and turns out Jessica inherited properties from her parents. I've sent officers to each location, but it could take some time. A lot of the buildings are motels and not in use. We're stretched with resources and warrants don't happen on the spot, so it's a process."

If I tell him I have her, will he stop looking? But what if Jessica has taken Benjamin to another one of her motels or properties? I don't know what's worse, having Dillon look for Benjamin or calling off the search and risking Jessica killing him. I can join the search, but having his resources will speed up the process. Fuck it.

At least if Dillon has him, then he'd be breathing and I could find a way to bargain for him. Take everyone Dillon loves if necessary.

"I need some reassurance," he grumbles, "and as much as I think you're an insane prick, Benny still beats you in the crazy factor, so I'm talking to you to keep him reeled in. If he goes around looking for her and shooting people, I will pull back my resources and turn them on hunting down him and you."

My spine straightens and fists clench. I don't take kindly to threats. This must be about Benjamin shooting his partner. "Your partner will live," I grind out.

"Not the fucking point," he snaps back.

"Fine, I'll keep Benjamin in line. Just hurry up and do your search."

The line dies and my eyes clash with Elizabeth. "Who

is Kami?" she asks.

"Why would you ask that?"

"I overheard you talking to him about her."

"Kami's not important," I lie smoothly. The stab of guilt from not only saying but feeling it is bearable, though. "I need to get you somewhere safe and cleaned up."

"*She* has him, doesn't she? The psycho blonde who had me?"

I offer a curt nod. Speaking the words aloud would only bring helplessness with them.

"It was my father. He did things." She shakes her head, her body trembling. I need to get her back to my place, fix her up, then come up with a plan. I know Jessica. Her persona, Lucy, is a sadist and she draws out her pleasure for days. We have some time, and Benjamin has endured worse than her.

"I'm going to pick you up and carry you to my car," I tell her softly. She's blinking rapidly. She's suffered emotional trauma, but like Benjamin, she's a survivor.

My hands slide beneath her legs, my warm skin clashing with the cold dewy feel of her own. I'm unprepared when she rests her head against my shoulder and places her small hand on my chest. Something inside me tightens and doesn't release. I know the possessive feeling all too well. Like Benjamin, I'm a collector of people too.

My suit jacket gapes over her small frame. The cuts on her chest are deep and weeping. She's going to need plastic surgery if she doesn't want horrendous scars. Her hair is wet and sticks to her face. Sad eyes find mine. She mourns him even though he still lives, but I know exactly what she's feeling. The thought of him not being here with us is an unbearable future.

With *us*.

I'll revisit that thought when I'm not going mad with worry.

"We will get him back," she whispers in understanding, looking straight into me, as if she sees something familiar.

What is it she sees?

Herself?

I dip the sponge in the tub and lift it to her head, squeezing the water so it runs down her hair and back. She's not shy in front of me. Her body is exposed to my eyes if I so wished to study it. And I do. Unapologetically. Her skin is delicate, like porcelain. It's no wonder Benjamin is so taken with her. She really is like a living doll. Impossibly long, dark lashes flutter like bat wings over her oval orbs. She's mesmerizing.

"I can treat your wounds, but once we have Benjamin safely back with us, I suggest we see a surgeon about those gashes," I offer, dropping the sponge and applying shampoo to her hair. My fingers knead her scalp, and she sighs into my touch.

"Thank you for finding me."

"It was Benjamin who gave himself up for that to be possible."

Her body tenses and the flickering in her eyes is far from innocent. She's slightly unhinged. Furious. Crazed. I marvel at how much she looks like her brother in this one moment. He, too, once gazed up at me from this bathtub, injured and in need of me.

Beautiful.

"I will kill her for this," she mutters, dark and determined.

It sends a thrill through my body and my skin begins to hum.

Her nostrils flare as she seems to lose herself to her thoughts. A familiar mania—one I've seen not only in Benjamin's eyes but my own—dances in hers. "I'll make her bleed and scream and beg. I'll make her wish her eyes never fell upon him or me." Her head tilts up so she can look directly at me again. Her teeth digging into her bottom lip before she says, "You can watch."

My stomach stirs, and I feel a change shifting inside me. I thought she would cause jealousy, wake up the demon within me, having it crave to eradicate her and feed on her until she was nothing. Because Benjamin only needs me. However, she has his same beauty inside her. The darkness—growing and flourishing inside her. Multiplying exponentially with each passing breath.

I want to harness it and sculpt it, just as I did him.

I want another monster.

I want her.

Fighting the smile that tugs at my lips, I stroke her cheek with my thumb and run it across her plump lip. She leans in to my affectionate touch. "I took the liberty of having someone pick up some clothes of yours," I tell her softly. I rinse her hair clean and offer her a towel. She stands and lets the water cascade down her body as though she's a water feature—one of a goddess—in a fountain. Aside from the damage on her chest, she's flawless.

Her skin is smooth and creamy, her deep brown hair long and dark enough to make her eyes pop.

Stepping into the towel, she wraps it around her body and once again places her hand on my chest over my heart. "Thank you."

The organ beats within its confines at her touch and I wonder if she'll notice that she's made me hard with a simple touch.

"Your clothes are in a bag on the bed. I'm going to take a shower."

"Okay." She smiles and holds my gaze as if she can see or feel the emotions I have burning through me for the person she loves. Instead of being jealous or angry, she's almost appreciative. Or better yet, hungry to dissect it. She's a monster too, after all.

I watch her sit on the unmade bed still in disarray from Benjamin and I earlier. I'm hypnotized by her as she strokes a palm over the mattress, gathering the sheet and bringing it up to her nose before wrapping it around her shoulders and laying down within it.

Can she smell him on them?

Can she smell us and what we did?

Does she know I love him too?

That we have something powerful and exhilarating as well?

My eyes close for a brief moment to gain some control back. All the emotions clawing inside me are too hard to convey with thoughts or words.

"What do I call you?" she pipes up from the bed, and I realize I haven't moved from my spot.

"What do you want to call me?" That answer is one I

give to most people, but she's not most people.

"What does *he* call you?"

All the names I've been given over the years dance on the tip of my tongue, so it surprises me how freeing it is to speak my given name to her. "Viktor. He calls me by my given name, Viktor."

She rolls the name around her mouth before sitting up. "I like Viktor. It's strong and alluring."

"Is it?" My voice is hoarse, and I wonder why I find myself hanging on to her every word. Her words are breathy and childlike. Musical in quality. They calm the fires within me. Perhaps she does the same for Benjamin.

"Go shower, Viktor," she says, her cheeks turning slightly pink. "We have our man to rescue."

I blink away my daze and stalk into the bathroom. Once I'm undressed, I turn the shower to the hottest setting. Stepping under the spray, I let the burn scorch away these crazy tormented thoughts racing around my mind. Seeing her, his precious doll, lying in the aftermath of us, was something otherworldly. The humming in my veins makes me sway on my feet. Taking my cock in hand, I stroke to the image, squeezing enough to cause pain, then releasing. I can't hold on to what I'm feeling, but I need to clear my mind so I can find him and bring him home.

When I finally step out of the bathroom, the room is empty. Drying off, I slip into a fresh suit, then find Elizabeth in the kitchen eating sandwich meat straight from the packet.

"Hungry?"

She shrugs her delicate shoulders. "She didn't feed me."

"What a disgraceful kidnapper," I scold in jest.

"Amateur, that's for sure." She's playful back. "Nice suit. Designer?" Her movements are graceful and fluid as she walks over to me. With a smile that makes my heart rate quicken, she strokes her fingers down the lapels. The heat of her body—and thank God for that, since not long ago she was on death's bed—warms my front. My cock stiffens in my slacks.

Her resilience and just the simple fact that she's my monster's doll is a turn on to the maximum degree.

"Tom Ford." I raise a brow, ignoring the way my body responds to hers. "And yours?" She's wearing a pretty dress that stops just above the knee with knee-high socks and plain Mary Janes.

"I make my own clothes. You'll have to let me make you something when all this is behind us." Her lashes fall against her cheeks that turn rosy.

Fucking beautiful little doll.

I hope she gets the chance to do just that. "I'd like that," I tell her honestly. My fingers touch her pouty mouth on their own accord. She doesn't move away. "But first, let's find this bitch."

She smiles against my fingers and her eyes brighten as if it's the best thing she's ever heard.

My thoughts flitter to the properties Dillon Scott informed me of. Jessica held our doll at one of those rundown motels, so it makes sense that she would take Benjamin to another property of hers. Although Dillon says he has officers checking them out, if I've learned anything from him, it's that he's useless. I'll have a better chance of finding Benjamin before him and won't have to risk Benjamin being taking into custody...*if he's still alive.*

He is. I'd feel it in my soul if anything had happened to him. We're parts of a whole, and when one part fades, the other parts sense the departure. I'd sense it. *She* would sense it.

Pulling my cell from my pocket, I call Luke. He can get me the same information Dillon has.

"I need every property listed for Jessica Johnson and her parents too, just in case," I tell him before ending the call. I find Monster's doll standing there looking up at me, just waiting for direction. "I need to go to the hospital and get Kami back."

Her smooth forehead crinkles at my statement.

"Who is Kami to you?"

The same question Dillon asked, and it's such a loaded question, I don't even know the answer anymore. But apparently, her curiosity won't simply go away. This doll wants answers—answers I don't even know how to explain. My thoughts drift to the past.

Her blood is warm on my knuckles and it looks so perfect smeared across her lips. Vlad will be pissed off that I drew blood, and she will be left with a fat lip before her registration, but the less she's worth, the more likely she is to survive. I want her to survive. More than that, I want to claim her as my bounty. She will be my perfect pet. Her thirst for violence is the sweetest thing I've ever tasted. Her labored breath is loud in the cramped cell as her exhausted body lies slumped against the wall. The small confines make the sparring so much more fun. Nowhere to run or hide— four walls to bounce her from.

"I win." I flash her a smirk and she wipes her hand

across her bleeding lip. "This time," she huffs.

"Every time," I correct, reaching forward and dragging her onto my lap.

"I'm going to hunt you in The V Games." Her body goes soft in my arms, as if she wants this every bit as much as I do.

"Not if I find you first."

Soft fingertips touch my face, jolting me back to the present. Monster's doll is on her tiptoes, smoothing out my furrowed brow with her delicate caress.

"You don't have to tell me if it's upsetting," she coos.

Taking her hands in mine, I offer her a small smile. "It's just that I'm not sure anymore, little doll. She saved me once."

"From who?"

I've only been in the arena for an hour and two people have already tried to kill me. It didn't make sense. Usually people were just finding their place and mapping out their route, the rooms they wished to visit, the fights they paid to fight in, the slaughter rooms they can unload their darkest fantasies within, but I became a target. And the price tag on my head must be substantial for people to bypass the main events at The V Games and come looking for their bounty instead. Usually sex and voyeurism were the starting games of choice, but now I have a night of trying to fend off a hit to look forward to.

Vlad, Vika, and my father will lose their minds over this.

The worst part is a hit ordered in here cannot be avenged outside The V Games. I am now free meat to be carved up by whoever has the biggest knife, and worse, it's for the person who has the biggest stack of cash. I don't have enemies, so the risk of a bounty on my head must be small. But not unheard of.

Plans of hunting down Kami and us going on a killing spree before fucking and beating her in front of the spectators is now a distant thought.

The game has changed.

"Someone I loved very much," I tell the little doll, who studies me with wide eyes as I reminisce. I keep bouncing to the past, like a rubber ball on the pavement.

Bounce. Soar. Bounce. Soar.

"Another woman?" she asks. My thoughts take me hostage with her question.

I've made it to the final countdown of the clock. The exit is within reach and the night of pleasure and mayhem is almost over. The time to prove to my father I can uphold his honor, survive, and enjoy in the spoils of the game he created for sinister men like us is coming to an end. Tonight's evening of hell proves our enemies are trying to invade us from the inside. It also shows our spectators there's conflict of a huge magnitude. Why else would there be a price on my head and so many vying to claim it? But with me making it to the end, it also proves you can't take down the Vasiliev clan.

We are monsters.

We are beasts.

We are unbreakable.

Blood layers my skin like a coat. My abs hurt and there are a few slashes deep enough to scar. The fight inside, however, is what is breaking me more than the fight on the outside. This is personal. Twenty-three assassination attempts

I've managed to survive and one of them came from a member of my father's staff. The man must have paid to enter The V Games for the sole purpose of doing someone else's bidding.

And I ended them all.

Our family created these dark games, therefore, we play them the best.

My soul deflates with the realization of whom could be behind this attempt. I saw him. *The night before The V Games at our home, leaving Vika's room, no doubt concocting a plan to betray me.*

Every ounce of training I'd had in my eighteen years of being a Vasiliev were put to action to fight off this flurry of new enemies set upon me by those I loved. By those I trusted.

Nothing.

No amount of training and preparation could have prepared me for such treachery, though, or the foreign feeling of intense sorrow that now clings to my soul. Twenty-three deaths to add to my tally—none for just the pleasure of it. And if it were not forbidden, hers *would be the twenty-fourth.*

My youth made me quick and gave me stamina over my opponents. The blade Vlad recommended was precise and deadly. Each session I'd had with Kami prepared me for brutal hand-to-hand combat, and I became their mistake. When they came for me, they fucking died.

"I'm sorry," I hear whispered into my ear from behind, a deep baritone of regret. My eyes close in resignation. I didn't hear anyone approach. I let my guard down so close to the end. I recognize that voice. Niko.

"She knows about us." Regret tightens his voice. *"She will tell your father and mine. We both can't have that, Viktor. If it's not me, it will be another. I'm sorry,"* Niko breathes, the pain evident in the cracking of his voice.

A humph resounds behind me as I wait to feel the blade pierce my skin, but nothing comes.

Turning, I'm shocked to find Niko on the ground, his blade by his side and Kami standing there with a baton. "Been having fun without me I see." She quirks a brow. *She's missing her clothes. Blood and bruises decorate her bare skin, and I stare at her dumbfounded. She's survived, and more than that, she fucking saved me.*

"I only knocked him out," she says with a grin. "Do you want to kill him?"

I look up to the clock and smile. Her eyes follow mine.

"Looks like we both win," she quips, her eyes dropping to the gates now lifting to signal the end of The V Games and the exit. Others move past us—an array of players carrying with them the loot of their night.

Reaching forward, I tug her toward me and lift her, throwing her over my shoulder. "No, I win, and you're my prize," I growl.

Vlad and Vika are waiting for me as I walk out. Vlad rushes toward me and pulls Kami from my shoulder before placing her on her feet. "Get her cleaned up and some medical attention," he orders to the team waiting to assist the victors. "Scan her code. She's Viktor Vasiliev's bounty. His attention turns my way. "Are you injured?" he asks me, but he already knows the answer. He would have been watching and going out of his mind with the need to join me in the fight for my life, otherwise.

"I didn't expect to be fending off so many attacks. How come Father didn't know the price on my head beforehand?" I demand, angry I wasn't informed my bounty would be so high.

"It wasn't the board," he assures me, and it confirms what I already assumed. "It was an outside bid sent direct to all assassins on the roster. We didn't know anything of it, Viktor."

I grit my teeth and motion with my head behind him. "Why don't we ask your dear friend and our sister's boyfriend who put a bounty on my head?"

Vika steps from the shadows like a prowling cat. "Rules of The V Games, brat. Contracts taken from inside the arena are not allowed. Revenge after The V Games ends is not allowed. It's what the entire foundation is built upon." She smiles, her eyes devious and dark. "V is not *for vengeance."*

"You've broken my heart, moya sestra," I reply, the fabric of who I am un-webbing at the seams.

"What is going on?" Vlad demands, darting his questioning gaze to our sister for answers she clearly has.

"Our brother is fucking what belongs to me," she hisses, then glares at me. "Thinking I don't know. That I can't smell you on him when he comes to me afterward. You're a disgrace to our father's name."

"So you try to have me killed, and worse, let Niko try to do it? I have bad news for you. He failed. You both failed. I'm still here. Now what? Are you just going to let him live and be a happy family knowing it's me he craves when he's deep inside you?" I taunt my twin.

Her face contorts, screwing up her pretty features in disgust. "You know me better than that, brat."

What?

She flicks her eyes to something behind me. Turning, I see Niko getting to his feet, clutching at his side. He's flanked by two men wearing head-to-toe leather, including masks, every inch covered in razor-sharp spikes. They look like fucking human hedgehogs.

The big ass monsters rush Niko before he can move or escape, spearing him between them. Like a tackle hug between football teammates. Rough. Brutal. Enthusiastic. The motherfucking razor twins laugh, sick and twisted and loud, as Niko is crushed between them. His eyes widen and blood drips from his mouth. The twins release him and have to use force to rip themselves away from his body. Flesh and crimson blood cling from their spikes. Niko lets out a pained groan before collapsing to the ground. His eyes are open and staring vacant up at me.

"I wanted him to see me as they killed him." Vika smirks, waving toward her dying boyfriend.

My blood boils. If it weren't for the rules, I'd push my knife right into the side of her throat and cut her wide open.

"Father won't like this one bit, Vika." Vlad grabs ahold of her shoulders, shaking her with unmasked fury. Vlad is always calm. Now, he's anything but. "What have you done?" he roars, his nostrils flaring with anger.

"He's not here, though, is he, brat?"

She's right. Why isn't Father here to congratulate me?

"You told him?" I choke.

This is bad. Fuck, this is bad.

Being gay or bisexual, not only in Russia, but in our family, is a disgrace. Unheard of even. Father knowing my sexual interests is the worst possible scenario.

"That his son fucks men?" she sneers. "Yes, Vik, we can't have you ruining everything for the rest of us. You've disgraced him."

I blink away the past and swallow down the bile in my throat.

My sister broke my heart when she betrayed me.

Father said I was damaging to the world he created for us. A poison in the veins of his empire. I was banished, stripped of my name, and given a new one.

A new life.

A new country.

A monster created from betrayal.

A master built from my own will to prove to my father he made a mistake forsaking me.

I press a kiss to the pretty doll's forehead and run my fingers through her silky brown hair as I seek comfort, the haunting memories still lingering. "We'll have story time for another day. Right now, we have shit to do."

The hospital is bustling with activity. Nurses and doctors flit around like worker bees while patients fill the waiting room and corridors. Monster's dolly refused when I tried to make her wait in the car for me. She gripped my hand so tight, her tiny nails marked the flesh. "Please don't leave me alone. I never want to be alone again." Her expressive eyes conveyed her conviction.

I agreed and brought her with me knowing it was a huge risk. But she's over eighteen and free to make her own choices. Even if Dillon finds out she's free, he can't take her. She has free will and she wouldn't want to leave her monster.

Or me.

The thought makes my chest ache.

I don't want her to leave me either.

Monster and Master are a packaged deal now.

We were from the moment I carried his big ass into my home and nursed him back to life. I breathed air back into the beast they tried to destroy by guns and fire.

You can't destroy men like Benjamin Stanton.

They destroy you.

"I need to know where a patient would be taken to if brought in by the police," I say smoothly to the skinny woman in blue scrubs standing behind the nurse station in the ER department.

She raises both brows and just stares at me like I'm an idiot.

When I say nothing else, she exhales heavily. "I can't tell you that information."

Fuck. Digging into my pocket, I pull out a stack of cash and push it toward her over the counter.

Her mouth drops open and she pushes it back at me. "You're kidding, right? This is a hospital. Now, please leave or I'll call security."

She will need it if she keeps being difficult. I'll wring her scrawny fucking neck.

"Viktor, come," my sweet Elizabeth urges as she ushers me down a corridor and slips into an office. "I know my mother's entry code and ID number. I can check the patients list from here." She smiles, her apple cheeks turning bright pink. Sitting down at the desk and booting up the computer, she looks so tiny. It makes me want to pluck her from the seat and have her sit in my lap instead. Naked. Grinding against my cock as I mark her pale flesh with my teeth. "Keep your eye on the door," she instructs, her tone fierce even though she's nothing but a little runt.

A smile graces my lips as I obey the demanding doll. Standing guard at the door, my eyes flicker between the entrance and her small hands as she flits them over the keyboard. Tiny hands that would look so good wrapped around my cock.

"Does she have a name that would be known?"

"Kami is all Dillon knows her by," I tell her, my voice gruff. "And he brought her in."

A few quiet minutes pass, then she looks up at me. "There is nothing of a Kami or even a patient brought in by a detective."

"Check for any patient with broken ankles, wrist, or lacerations," I coach.

My heart ticks along with the clock above the pretty dolly's head. Benjamin doesn't have time for us to be hunting down fucking Kami. I should just make Dillon bring her to me. Maybe he took her to a different hospital.

"She's not in the database. Are you sure it's this hospital?"

"Check for a Josey, also brought in by a detective."

She once again taps her fingers over the keys.

"Yes. Josey Manuel. She has cuts and bruises, but has already been discharged."

"Come on, let's get out of here," I grunt.

Her small frame rushes over to me, and when we exit, we almost collide with a doctor.

"Elise, how are you? You've changed. Nice outfit." The woman smiles awkwardly. I'm debating strangling her and stuffing her in the file cabinet inside the office we just left when Elizabeth pipes up.

"Oh, I know, right? I'm just here to visit the kiddies in the sick ward. It looks good on my résumé to do charity work." She smacks her lips together like she's chewing on gum and twirls a strand of her hair.

"That's so selfless of you." The woman rolls her eyes and hurries off without a goodbye.

"Quite the actress," I compliment her. Visions of her acting on camera for her site assault my mind.

In her pretty little dress.

With her hand in her pretty frilly panties.

Sweet moans that just beg to be turned into screams.

Fuck, that's a good image.

CHAPTER THIRTEEN

~ Pulverized ~

Benny

It's been a long time since I've slept so deeply. My eyes slowly blink open and I find myself spread-eagle on top of a pool table in some warehouse. It's cold and damp and I'm naked.

Fucking cunt is going to suffer for this.

Does she not understand who it is she's goading? She can do whatever she wants and I'll still survive. Then, I'll make her pleasure cuts look like papercuts compared to what I will inflict on her. I'll bleed her out and stitch her back up just to bleed her out again and again and again.

"Jess," I roar.

My eyes scan the pallets surrounding me. Shoe boxes. No, skate boxes.

"It's a solid plan, you must admit that," she croons from somewhere out of sight.

She wants my approval. My motherfucking admiration.

She's more likely to get tears from me than that. And tears are never going to happen. Viktor is the only living soul who's ever witnessed such a sight.

"I thought it was poetic that we finish where it all could have started," she says in a dreamy way. "Why didn't you want to come that day?"

She has more issues than my father abusing her. Who holds onto something so petty? She's mediocre at best. Her revenge is pathetic, like her fake tits. "I talked Cassian into killing your father," she divulges. "Told him details of how he should have it done too."

I doubt that. Viktor would not take a lead from anyone, let alone her.

"Stop trying to pretend you have power where you don't," I snort, mocking her.

She creeps out from the shadows like a snake slithering up next to me, her knife in hand. My cock is bigger. Dragging the blade down my throat where old burn scars litter the expanse of skin, she digs in, opening up the flesh.

I grin up at her, knowing she was hoping for a whine. Fuck her.

"I knew you'd have a high threshold for pain," she breathes, her voice wispy as her eyes glass over. "Why did you have to come back into my world? This wasn't something I'd planned, until I saw you and remembered who you were."

I'm already bored and hope she will start causing real damage so I can at least pass out from the pain and get a reprieve from her goddamn mouth.

"It was as if," she says softly, "as if you wanted to come and take everything away from me again."

"What the fuck are you talking about? I don't care about you at all. You're not even on my radar. You are a speck of dust in the desert to me. Irritating when it goes in your eye. That's it."

The blade runs across my pectoral and onto my torso. She carves and whispers the word she's creating. "Cunt."

Meh, tell me something I don't know, whore.

"It took me years, years to find a place in his heart."

Whose heart? Jesus fucking Christ. She means Viktor. She's in love with Viktor. My lungs inflate and deflate with the knowledge. The burning pain offers a diversion to the rage exploding within me at the thought of her and Viktor together.

"You really are deluded. You think you're worthy of him?" I taunt.

More cutting low across my stomach. Hurts like a motherfucker.

"Liar," she murmurs as she carves the word, ignoring my question.

"Why would you ever think he would be interested in a fake, scarred up whore like you?" I goad louder.

She lifts the blade and screams as she plunges it into my thigh.

Jesus Christ!

I yell internally, holding my breath to try to deal with the agony. My nostrils flare as I suck in air.

"It's because of you!" she screams. "Once you came, he couldn't see anything or anyone else. You took him from me, like you stole my life when I was a kid."

My fucking father has a lot to answer for. If he weren't already dead, I'd skin him alive him for this shit.

The silence descends, becoming more violent than rage. That's when the true fury washes over and takes the fear of consequences away.

"Do you believe in fate, Monster?" she murmurs. "How can you not when our worlds once again clashed like this?"

I glare up at her. "So, let me just clarify what's happening," I say, taking some deep breaths. It's freezing in here and I'm struggling to stop my bones from rattling. "You are mad because I turned you down years ago, then Cassian preferred to idolize my cock over your pussy? So, it's rejection that's the real issue—nothing to do with some old man finding by some miracle pleasure in that cesspool you call a pussy?"

"Asshole," she bellows, jumping onto the table and straddling me. Her eyes are wild, her nostrils flaring. Her fake tits bulge from her leather cat suit. "Oh, you don't like my pussy, Monster?" She shrieks like a rabid animal. Feral and crazed. Reaching between her legs, she grips my flaccid cock. If she takes the knife to it, I will eat her face off. Her hands are cold, and she begins stroking me. A laugh rumbles from my chest.

"Are you trying to make it shrivel up and fall off?"

Leaning forward, she holds the knife to my throat. "Oh, it will do just the opposite actually. Let's see how much you enjoy this."

Getting to her feet beside the pool table, she places the blade down on the edge and unzips her stupid outfit. What the fuck is she doing? Her tits stand from her chest like two mountain peaks chasing down a narrow waist. Her pussy is bold and tattooed with a flower of some sort.

"Am I supposed to be turned on by that, freak show?" I ask in a bored tone. My blood is congealing on my skin. I want this over with.

Straddling my thighs, she takes my dick into her mouth and slurps. She's literally a pro at this. Spent a lot of her younger days working the front of The Vault. Always had clients' dick and balls in her ugly mouth, so she knows how to get a desired reaction. When I feel the blood pumping there, I yank against the restraints, pulling at them to try to free myself. "Get your disgusting mouth off me," I growl.

"Gladly," she purrs.

She reaches for something she placed near my feet. It's her cell phone. She crawls up my legs and situates herself above my dick that she's woken against its wishes. Holding her phone out with one hand and taking my dick in her other, she lowers her vulgar cunt around my shaft.

"Don't fucking do it, whore," I bellow, yanking and trying to free myself.

"Damn," she gasps, sitting fully down on my cock. Her eyes roll back as she begins rocking her hips. "I knew this would feel good."

"I'm going to fucking gut you from slit to slit and empty you out," I roar.

Her moans are more of madness than pleasure as she continues to move and film herself. "What will your dolly and Cassian think when I send them this video of you fucking me?"

She's insane.

"They'll like the one of my coming all over your entrails when you're dead a whole lot fucking better," I hiss.

I hate how my goddamn body reacts. This bitch gets my dick hard and I have no control. It's not my body lighting up for her; it's purely manipulation.

"Oh," she moans as she leans forward, her blonde hair curtaining around us. "Yesss…"

Her hooded eyes are locked on mine as she fucks me. My body thrums and pulsates with the need to come. I have no attraction to this woman whatsoever. I never have. All that burns through me is hate for her. Her hips rotate and rock. Even though her cunt is loose, I know I'll come soon.

I don't pretend I'm with Viktor or Bethany to escape.

Instead, I keep them safe and get turned on by my hate for this bitch. My dick is impossibly hard at the idea of her blood spattered all over this room. I want to scalp her and bring her filthy hair back to make a wig for my dolly, then order her to burn it.

"You like this too," she whimpers.

I buck my hips into her, but not for the reasons she thinks. With each yank of my arms and legs, the bindings loosen. The phone in her hand clatters to the table as she finds her fake breasts and touches them.

Her body starts to tremble as her orgasm nears. With a roar, I rip my right arm from the rope and seize her neck. A garbled sound escapes her when I yank her to me. My hand crushes her throat and she flails her arms around her.

Her face turns purple.

Prettiest she's ever looked.

When her eyes seem as though they'll pop from her skull, I come. Fuck, do I come. The thought of her death is fucking delightful. My seed pours into her, hot and furious. She's seconds from passing out.

Slash!

Fire screams across my forearm, and my grip on her lessens. It's enough for her to jerk free of my hold. Her body makes a popping sound as she scrambles off my dick.

"You almost killed me!" she screams, waving her bloody knife in front of her as she slides off the table and out of reach.

"Come here and I'll finish the job, dirty slut!" I bellow back.

Her body trembles as she frantically looks around the room for something. With my arm free, I try to reach over to untie my left one. I'm still tugging when she sneaks up behind me, pinches my nose shut, and shoves a pill down my throat. I gag as it slides down, but manage to punch the shit out of the side of her head while simultaneously biting her fingers.

The knife clatters to the floor and her body crashes into some boxes.

Then, silence.

I grunt as I tug some more at the rope. The room is already starting to spin. Once I manage to free my other arm, which takes time—too much time—I sit up and force a finger down my throat. Bile spews from me, but the pill has already started taking its effect.

Desperate to get the fuck out of here, I work quickly on my ankles. I manage to loosen one, but then everything turns and closes in around me. My arm becomes heavy as my fingers swipe at the rope, but I lose focus and can't make contact. My vision blurs and the heavy air begins weighing down on me.

No!

The storm clouds are rolling in.

Darkness.

Okay, Viktor, so I take my thoughts back. I need you to come save my ass. This bitch is fucking crazy...

Black.

CHAPTER FOURTEEN

~ Riven ~

Dillon

"You two look fucking cozy," I snap, running my fingers through my greasy hair. I haven't showered today, but that's because I've been at the hospital. When I'm not trying to comfort my wife and enjoy our new son, Mason, I'm trying to locate Elizabeth and take down psychos.

I need a goddamn vacation.

Maryann came straight to the hospital from the airport and hasn't left since. She bounces back between her daughter in Jade's room and doing her job in order to keep her mind off the fact that one of her children has been taken.

Marcus stiffens, but makes no moves to remove his hand from Elise's bare thigh. The dress she's wearing has ridden up now that she's curled against his side asleep. Jade is also asleep while Mason is in the nursery for a few hours.

He stretches out his long legs and winces, the bullet hole no doubt hurting. His thumb runs a comforting circle on her skin. "I'm going to make an honest woman out of her. We had a long talk earlier. She was wrong for lying, but our feelings for each other are real." He sighs. "I love her."

I grit my teeth. Marcus could be her fucking dad he's so old. Probably better suited for her mother. Elise is barely nineteen. A damn kid. And now, she's carrying his kid. I've always thought of myself as a big brother of sorts to the twins. Big brothers can kick their little sister's boyfriend's ass, right? What about murder?

My thoughts drift to Elizabeth.

They were together. Benny and Elizabeth. Siblings. Sick as fuck.

God, I have to find her and save her from that monster.

"While you were napping," I grit out, changing the subject from his inappropriate love for Elise, "Swanson called. The Stanton's neighbor, Phil Lawrence, was found in a ditch."

Marcus's eyes widen. "I still can't believe they didn't kill us. I take it they did kill Phil Lawrence, though?"

"Multiple stab wounds in the abdomen hitting every vital organ with precision. It doesn't seem to be the work of Benny…" I trail off, scrubbing at my scruffy cheeks. I've yet to tell him the shit I'm doing on the side to get Elizabeth back. He's my partner and I should, but I refrain. "Definitely a professional."

"Cassian Harris. Too fucking cool and collected. I knew that asshole had a backstory. We got anything on him yet?" he asks.

Elise stirs, makes a whimper sound, but then calms when he strokes her hair. Okay, so maybe he is good for her. Elise needs a grown up in her life to take care of her. As much as Maryann tried, those girls were doomed the moment their daddy shot his seed into her womb.

"Nothing. He's too clean. We can't find shit on him."

"Apart from harboring a wanted felon," Marcus adds, but he knows as well as I do a man of Harris's wealth will get a topnotch lawyer to find some loophole bullshit and he will walk. Even the death of the other club owner, Mr. Law. Everything points to Harris, but the evidence is too circumstantial.

My eyes drift over to Jade. She's angelic when she sleeps. Thank fuck our son is okay. My heart aches because I haven't seen MJ since this morning when my mom brought her by. Mom hates the fact that I have two uniforms following her, my niece, Jazzy, and MJ around everywhere, but I can't take any chances.

"What about Jessica Johnson? Any new info?"

Aside from what I already told him—her parents owning a shitload of properties we're investigating—nothing. "Nope. Have you talked to Josey?"

"She texted earlier to check in from the safe house we put her in. Apparently Duncan is hitting on her," he grumbles. "That asshole has no clue. She's into chicks, not dicks."

I smirk. "You sure Duncan has a dick? I mean, has it even been confirmed?"

We both chuckle, a momentary reprieve from the stress.

He eventually yawns and Elise wakes up. Their eyes meet, both of them smiling. I can't even be pissed when they look at each other like that—like how Jade looks at me. Besides, I have bigger fish to fry.

"You think you can keep an eye on my wife while I run and make a stop? You're crippled anyway," I tease as I stand and stretch. I feel like shit and could sleep for a week. Instead, I'll dope up on more coffee and keep burning at both ends until I have all these psychos locked up and Elizabeth back.

"I've got this." He pulls his department issued piece from his pocket and holds it up. "Now, whatever it is you think you might have a lead on, go fucking sniff it out."

I give him a clipped nod. Am I that transparent to my partner? At least he supports my desire to do whatever it takes to get Elizabeth back. Now that he's with Elise, I can see how he'd see this as a family matter.

You take care of family no matter what.

Empty. Empty. Empty.

Every time a detective calls to tell me they've checked a new property and it's clean, I die a little inside.

Where the fuck are they?

Walking the hospital corridor, the stench of loss and misery cloud around me. Maryann proved what I'd learned from Jade, and that's that mothers had more strength than anyone I'd ever known.

How she can still be holding it together and working is beyond me, but she's been taking care of Kami in an isolated, police-protected part of the hospital. Anything to keep her mind off the disappearance of her daughter.

Benny did this to Kami, and although Harris had some sway over him, it wasn't enough for Benny to free her. When he finds out she's gone, he may come looking for her. That fucker doesn't leave loose ends.

Jade was a loose end.

My heart clenches and I drive that thought away. He's moved on to other shit. She's not even on his radar anymore.

I hope.

It doesn't matter, though. I won't allow him to hurt another woman on my watch. Not Jade. Not Elizabeth. Not Kami. Fuck no. I already feel dirty just by helping him. In reality, though, I'm not helping him, I'm searching for Elizabeth, which I'd be doing anyway.

Scrubbing my hands down my face, I ignore the churning in my gut telling me I'm hungry. Time is ticking by, and for all we know, and what statistics tell me, the window for finding her alive is closing.

"Dillon?" Maryann gently asks from behind me.

"Hey," I greet. "I just came to see if Kami is ready to talk yet."

She nods in confirmation and leads me to her room. "She's on heavy painkillers, so talk slow and give her time to formulate and convey a reply."

"Thanks. I will."

Pushing open the door, I realize the room is large and dark apart from a dim overhead light over Kami's bed. Tubes run into her veins on her arm, feeding her medication. Both feet are in casts and elevated. A cast also stretches from her wrist to elbow, and her face is a myriad of blue and purple bruising. I want to ask how she's feeling, but it's a stupid fucking question—one Jade hates being asked.

"Are you comfortable?" I opt for instead.

Water builds in her eyes, and she makes a weird snort sound. Her eyes turn to look away from me, but her mouth parts. "I n-never thought he c-could do this t-to me. To us," she chokes out.

Who does she mean?

"Can you tell me what happened?"

Her body trembles. "I was betrayed."

"By Benjamin Stanton?"

Her nose crinkles and the tears spill onto her cheeks. "Viktor," she whispers, her features contorting in pain, as if saying the name physically hurts. Her chest lifts with the force of her grief. "Viktor chose him." She sounds so broken, nothing like the girl I first saw at The Vault.

"Who is Viktor?"

Her eyes ignite at that question, and her brow line collapses. "I need a phone," she says, determination making her try to sit up in her bed.

"Don't move. You'll only hurt yourself. Here," I say, offering my cell phone. She snatches it and looks to the door.

Fine, I can take a hint.

Moving from the room and closing the door behind me, I stay right outside, pinning my ear to the thin wood separating us to try to hear any of the conversation. When she exhales heavily, I hear her clearly. Maryann joins me out of curiosity, and she too pins her head to the door. There's silence, then words.

"Vlad, eto Klara. U Viktora nepriyatnosti. On poteryal svoy razum. Eto ne chelovek, eto monstr. He needs you."

"Is that Russian?" I whisper, and Maryann nods.

The conversation falls quiet. Maryann pulls away first and rushes over to the nurse station. Quickly, she scribbles something down, then hands it to me.

Vlad, it's Klara. Viktor is in trouble. He's lost his will to another. A man, a monster."

"I speak Russian," she announces, and the fact that my mouth parts in shock has her rolling her eyes in a way that reminds me of Elise.

"I speak five languages. It's important with all the medical conferences I have to take part in all over the world."

So, who the hell is Viktor? This has to be Harris. He goes by many names. He doesn't have an accent, though. Fuck. Why is everything so cryptic and complicated?

With a heavy sigh, I knock on the door before stepping inside.

"Kami, let me help you and keep you safe. Can you tell me who Viktor is? I can protect you from Benjamin Stanton."

She hands me back my cell phone and weakly smiles. "He won't be a problem for much longer."

"What does that mean?"

Anger flashes in her eyes, but then she closes them, as if to hide the glint. "I'm tired. I want to sleep."

Perfect. More of nothing.

Leaving her to rest, I call Reeves along the way.

"Sir?" He answers on first ring.

"Tell me you still have Jacob. If not, bring him back in. I need him for something."

I hang up after he confirms and find Maryann jotting down information in a medical file as I approach her. "I need to leave the hospital for a little while."

She frowns. "Okay. Do you have a lead on my daughter?" Hope, albeit brief, flickers in her eyes.

"Possibly," I lie. "I'm going to have Jade moved down here. Only you are permitted to treat her."

"Of course. Go find my girl and I'll take care of yours."

Coming into the precinct, I'm met with concern over Jade and congratulations. As much as I want to revel in the fact we have a son, I can't. Benny is once again ruining everything for us.

"Reeves," I bark, and he jog towards me.

"Sir, Jacob is in interview room one."

I pull out the note Harris gave Josey. I'd already slipped it into a bag when I took it from her. "I need you to take this to the lab. We need dermatoglyphics. I want prints pulled stat. Tell them I need this rushed. It takes priority over everything."

"Okay, sir. On it."

Making my way to interview room one, I open the door and signal for Jacob to follow me. "I want you to do your hacking thing and to delve deep. Uncover everything you can on Cassian Harris. Go over his history with a fine-tooth comb. All documentation that makes him a US citizen. Scrutinize everything and look for inconsistencies and forged information."

I point to the seat at my desk, and he snorts at my software.

"If you want me to do this, I'll need my equipment,

and I'll need to be paid for the hours."

"How about I just don't throw you back in jail?"

"If you want me to do good work, then you need to start sweetening the pot."

Motherfucker.

"Fine. I'll speak to the department head and see what I can do. In the meantime, I'll get Reeves to take you to retrieve everything you need from your place. But this is time sensitive. Meaning, the faster you get me this information, the more rewarding I'll be feeling."

I nod our agreement and shoot a message to Reeves with instructions. My cell lights up after I hit send.

"Yes?"

"It's Harris," he says, his voice cold. "I have something. I need you to meet me."

Me. Not us. "Where's Benny?"

"He's busy. I need back up. Can you meet me or not?"

Not. I smell a trap.

When I don't reply, he lets out a ragged sigh. A chink in his otherwise impenetrable armor. "Listen, this is important."

"Fine, but if this is some sort of tri—"

"I'll text the location," he cuts me off, then hangs up.

I stare down at the cell wanting to reach through it and break his jaw. The address he sends is one I saw earlier. I quickly check the last place out on our database, and sure enough, it's one of Jessica's family's properties. I confirm with our teams to see whether it's been searched yet.

"No, it's on the list, sir."

"Okay, thank you." I end the call, and despite my better judgment, leave to meet Harris. Alone.

As soon as I pull into the parking lot of the dilapidated motel, I notice right away one of the doors is open on the second floor and there are no other cars here. My heart rate picks up as I exit my vehicle and draw my weapon. I creep upstairs and sneak into the room. It's pitch black and I don't hear any voices or breathing. Just dripping.

Drip.

Drip.

Drip.

I pull out my flashlight and illuminate the room. It's dirty and trashed, but someone's been here recently. Blood coats the mattress, and it still looks wet. I walk over and inspect the mess. Definitely fresh. On the floor, in a shredded heap, is a once frilly dress. A familiar dress. Fuck.

I yank out my phone and dial the precinct. "I need all units to the Crystalline Hotel, room twenty-six. Get the CSI here stat. The crime scene is fresh." I grit my teeth. "Looking at a possible homicide."

Once I hang up, I swallow down my emotion. Elizabeth can't be dead. Sure, there's a fuck-ton of blood, but she's a fighter. I'll find her and bring her home.

My phone rings, and I answer it on the first chime. "What?"

A chuckle. Cold and empty. "Detective Scott."

"Cassian Harris."

"Plans have changed," he bites out.

A sickness roils in my belly. I shouldn't have drank so much bitter hospital coffee. "I came here like you asked, asshole. Whose blood is this?" I bark out.

He chuckles. "I got to her first."

"Elizabeth." I stiffen and let out a growl. "Is she alive?"

"Barely. So much blood, Detective."

"I'm coming to get her," I snap. "She needs medical attention."

"I need something from you first," he says, his voice smooth and unaffected. No wonder he and Benny get along so fucking well. They both came from the same loony bin.

"I don't negotiate with madmen. I already helped you once. I helped Kami." I don't tell him how much she could have possibly helped me with finding out who the real Harris is.

"I need a list of all the properties Jessica Johnson's family owns. Now," he barks, his cool persona slipping at the mention of Kami's name.

"I'm already culling through them, dumbass," I snarl. "What the fuck do you think I've been doing? And if you have Elizabeth, what does it matter?"

I hear whimpering in the background. Crying. Goddammit.

"D-Dillon," Elizabeth sobs, her voice violently shaking. "H-Help m-me."

"Shhh," I coo, my heart hammering in my chest. "I'm going to get you, sweetheart. Hang tight. Can you tell me where you are?"

A bloodcurdling scream deafens me.

"LEAVE HER ALONE!" I bellow.

"You get me Jessica Johnson. Alive."

"Is this some revenge bullshit?" I roar.

"She has something of mine," he snaps. "And I want it

back. You're going to help me get it back."

The flashlight in my hand hits the mirror, the word "revenge" painted on it in blood. There is a fuck more to this story I don't know.

"I'll help you," I tell him, my voice cold. "Let me talk to her." The moment she gets back on the line, I try to calm her. "I'm coming to get you, sweetheart. Just hang in there."

I trot out of the room and down the stairs to wait on the units. I need to get back to my car so I can try to put a trace on this call. I'm almost to the door when something hard presses into my back.

"Help me," Elizabeth pleads into the phone. "Please, Dillon. I need you."

"Keep walking," Harris growls from behind me.

Fuck!

If he's here, Elizabeth is close. With the phone still pressed to my ear, I let him walk me around the side of the building. When my eyes lock with Elizabeth's, a breath of air is expelled from my chest. But the moment I really get a good look at her, I suddenly can't breathe at all.

She's dressed like a little fucking doll.

Pretty hair and makeup.

No tears at all. No distress.

A motherfucking accomplice.

Harris yanks my cuffs from my belt and tosses them to Elizabeth.

"Cuff him, doll."

She beams and bounces forward, her dress blowing in the wind. I'm so stunned, I don't have words. Harris's gun will shatter my spine if I fight him and he gets a shot off. Fuck.

"Sorry, D," she says softly, "but we really do need your help, and this is just a precaution. Viktor says you don't like him," she whispers for only me to hear, and my brain might explode at the revelation of her calling him by that name. So, Viktor *is* his real name? There's not an ounce of Russian in his speech. Maybe he was raised here.

The cuffs snap together and my hands are now shackled behind me. She takes the phone and turns it off before regarding me sadly. Her lips purse together in a pout. "She has him."

"Benny?" I ask, my tone incredulous.

"We have to save him," she says, her eyes filling with tears.

Harris guides me over to an SUV and lifts the hatch. He shoves me inside and taps my skull with his gun. The motherfucker looks smooth and composed in a fancy-ass suit Marcus would love. Not a damn hair out of place. "Good dog," Harris says, his grin wolfish. "You comply and this all ends well, my family for your family."

I blink in horror when he curls an arm around Elizabeth and pulls her to his side. He kisses the top of her head and she beams at me.

"I really don't want anything to happen to Jade and the kids," she says softly. "This isn't about them, I promise. But you need to help us, then we can all be happy." She bites on her bottom lip and frowns. "Don't mess up, Dillon. I couldn't bear it if something happened to them."

Jade. My kids.

A threat.

"What the hell do you want?" I demand. "I'm not helping you find that monster."

"I want Kami back. Where is she?" Harris barks.

I wasn't expecting that. "She's injured. She can't go anywhere with you."

He growls. "I have people who can take care of her."

"What about Benny?" I taunt. "He doesn't seem that fond of her."

"Don't you worry about them," he tells me, his voice calculating and calm. "Worry about your own family."

Fuck.

Fuck.

Fuck.

"Think about it," he adds.

Then closes the hatch.

Fuck.

CHAPTER FIFTEEN

~ *Split* ~

Elizabeth

VIKTOR EVENTUALLY MOVED DILLON TO the back seat, and Dillon has been quiet ever since, which makes me nervous. He'd rattled out Kami's location, revealing she was in fact at the hospital, just in a different part, surrounded by armed officers. Dillon made it clear we won't be able to get her, but then he's been eerily silent.

As we drive quietly, I can't help but notice how much pain I feel. My chest hurts from the cuts, but the one that's the deepest is inside. Benny traded himself for me.

He loves me.

When I feel Viktor's eyes on me, I peek over at him under my lashes. He's handsome. Like every bit as good looking as Benny, but different. Maybe scarier in some ways, but more refined. As though he's had years of practice hiding his monsters, where Benny's roam freely.

I shouldn't trust him, but I do.

His eyes don't lie.

The amber flames blaze any time I mention Benny. Love and admiration and need. It makes me curious. I want to crawl into his lap and stare into his honey orbs—to ask him questions about my elusive lover. If anyone knows things about Benny, it's Viktor. They're close, I can feel it in my bones.

"Why would she want him?" I suddenly ask. She said revenge, but didn't elaborate.

"She's bitter," Viktor mocks. "Benjamin refused to go skating with her."

"So, this Jessica Johnson has Benny because he turned her down?" Dillon decides to speak, his question asked in an incredulous tone.

"Yes. Did I slur?" Viktor snaps back.

I flinch at his harsh tone.

"And did she mention the skating, or did he?" Dillon asks.

"She mentioned it," Viktor replies. "Why?"

I glance back at Dillon. His eyes narrow. "Because it must hold more significance."

Viktor clenches the steering wheel and a muscle in his neck ticks. "She blames him for what Stanton did to her after he left. He picked her up and raped her."

Like a tennis match, my gaze darts back to Dillon.

Dillon widens his eyes. "I didn't see that fucking coming, but I'm not surprised. That motherfucker hurt so many women..." he trails off when he realizes he's talking shit about my father. After clearing his throat, he announces, "There's a property she acquired after her inheritance."

Viktor jerks his head back so violently, I'm afraid he'll run us into a ditch. "What?"

Dillon nods.

Viktor slams on the brakes and pulls out his phone. I lean over to watch as he scrolls through some links a guy named Luke sent him, finding the one that says "Ace Roller Shack" and highlighting it.

"Motherfucker. The goddamn roller shack," he breathes in disbelief. "She owns it." He flashes me a brilliant smile that makes my thighs clench. "She has to have taken him there." His large hand reaches over, lacing his fingers with mine. "We're going to get him back. And we're going to fucking end her."

My heart does a somersault.

"I can't wait."

CHAPTER SIXTEEN

~ *Slivered* ~

Viktor

I PULL UP TO THE building in desperate need of repair. Or a fucking match. It's a hellhole trapped in the late eighties or early nineties. There is a car here. Not hers, but someone's.

"I want you to wait here," I tell our doll.

"No," she immediately barks in response before opening the car door.

Bad dolly.

I grab her hand to stop her fleeing, enjoying the way electric energy seems to pulse between us. Her gaze tears from mine and she frowns as she inspects the building through the windshield.

"But you know what? It's too quiet," she murmurs. "What if she killed him?"

I pull her to my side over the console and hug her, ignoring the disgusted grunts coming from the backseat. "Benny isn't dead," I assure her as I inhale her sweet scent. "I can feel it. Don't you feel it?"

"This is some psychotic bullshit," Dillon mutters under his breath.

Elizabeth nods and lets out a sigh of relief. She lifts her head to stare at me, her plump, kissable lips parted. I want to suck on her bottom one. "You're right."

"Okay, you can come with me," I concede as I get out the car, never tearing my gaze from her arresting features. Her eyes light up and she smiles at me bright enough to illuminate the darkened parking lot. I wink at her before stepping over to open the back door. Dillon scoots toward me, and I grin at him. "You're waiting here." I smack the butt of my gun against his temple, hard enough to knock his big ass out, and enjoy the hum of pleasure when he falls against the seat.

Keeping my gun aimed and our doll tucked behind me, I creep along the building, trying the doors. None give under my hand, and I'm debating smashing a window when she tugs on my sleeve. I watch with interest as she pulls something from her hair and jams it in the door lock. "I saw this done on YouTube once." She smiles, jimmying the lock. Well, damn. She *is* perfect. Her mouth pops open with wonder when she tries the handle and it opens.

There's silence stretched out before us inside before a loud crash interrupts it.

Fuck.

I hope we're not too late.

Picking up speed, my feet carry me toward the sound. There are a set of double doors open and leading into what looks like the warehouse situated at the back of the roller rink. Elizabeth's body collides into the back of mine when I stop suddenly.

Benjamin lies slumped on the floor, his foot raised at an awkward angle, rope keeping his ankle bound to a pool table while his body has fallen from it.

He's naked and bleeding. Open wounds oozing.

Rushing to his side, I check for a pulse. It's there and steady.

Thank fucking God.

"Unbind his foot," I order, and she obeys, yanking at the rope.

"It's all right," she coos. "We're here. We have you."

Freeing him, Elizabeth drops down next to me and studies the cuts and slurs marring is flesh.

"That whore," she breathes.

It's then I realize Jessica is here somewhere. A groaning sound echoes behind us, and both Elizabeth and I get to our feet to seek out who it belongs to.

Jessica lies sprawled out amongst the crates holding boxes. One of the boxes has torn open and roller skates litter the floor around her. She's also naked, and there's signs of intercourse smeared on her spread thighs.

"She raped him," I snarl in shock.

Elizabeth's eyes expand and dart to mine. A wailing sound rips from her, almost deafening. Her body jolts forward, racing toward Jessica. I start after her, but stop when she picks up a skate and straddles Jessica.

Smash!
Smash!
Smash!

I watch in sick satisfaction as Elizabeth crushes Jessica's face with the four wheels of the roller skate. Bone crunches. Groans of pain escape our doll's victim. Blood splatters.

"You fucking whore!" she screams as a spray of

crimson explodes around her. I lean in closer to discover Jessica's face is no longer recognizable. Just a hole in her skull of meat and bones and blood.

Smash!
Smash!
Smash!

Grabbing Elizabeth from behind, I drag her reluctantly from Jessica's body. Crimson beauty decorates every inch of her skin and clothes. She's magnificent, and I'm bewildered by this intense need to claim her. I want to tear her frilly panties away and sink my cock deep inside her while I kiss her bloody mouth.

"Benjamin needs us," I tell her when she stares at me, the same fire in my eyes shining bright in her gaze.

My cock jolts as I wonder if she's imagining a similar scenario.

Her tense body relaxes and she nods. "Okay."

I help her to her feet, then hoist Benjamin over my shoulder. Our beautiful bloody doll leads the way out of the building, the roller skate still clutched in her hand as though she may need to use it again. Before we step outside, I grab her wrist and force her to shake the skate from her grip. It falls into an empty box. I'll send men to burn this shit to the ground, including the murder weapon.

"Pull Dillon out," I instruct when we near the vehicle outside.

She opens the car door and begins dragging Dillon's still knocked-out ass onto the pavement. Her chest rises and falls with the effort, gasps escaping her as she struggles. He eventually drops to the asphalt, and she beams up at me.

I should kill him, but sirens blare in the distance, which means we need to go.

His family for mine. Surely he won't forget my threat.

She climbs into the backseat and motions to her lap. "Here, let me hold him." Her eyes are filled with love and strength, even if she does look like something out of a nightmare with bits of flesh and blood coating her pretty porcelain face. Leaning in, I deposit him into the backseat, and she pulls his head onto her thighs, stroking her sticky fingers through his hair as she mumbles a song.

Miss Polly had a dolly who was sick, sick, sick.
So she phoned for the doctor to be quick, quick, quick.
The doctor came with his bag and his hat,
And he knocked at the door with a rat-a-tat-tat.
He looked at the dolly and he shook his head,
And he said, "Miss Polly, put her straight to bed!"
He wrote on a paper for a pill, pill, pill,
"I'll be back in the morning, yes I will, will, will."

What a beautiful sight, my monster and his doll, reunited. They're mine and I am theirs. Stalking over to the open door of the roller rink, I pull a lighter from my pocket and hold it to one of the dusty boxes just inside the door. There's no time to call for my men to clean up the scene. This'll have to do.

The flames pouring from the doorway are a beautiful sight as I stare at them in my rearview mirror.

Time to take my family home.

CHAPTER SEVENTEEN

~ Burst ~

Benny

SHE'S ON TOP OF ME, her disgusting cunt taking what doesn't belong to her. My skin burns and screams in protest of movement, but I need to get her off me.

Kill her.

End this.

Rage courses through me, giving me strength. Bolting up with a roar, the room spins and seems to expand.

She's not on top of me. I'm not in that place. My precious Bethany's face replaces Jess's.

"Oh, you're awake," she cries out. "Viktor come quick."

My head swims and I want to hold her, to pull her against me, but she's staying back. Why?

Viktor appears next to her and he sighs. "It's a relief to see those mean brown eyes, Monster." He smiles, taking Bethany's hand in his and squeezing. I don't miss the way she beams up at him like he's the fucking king of her world. He has that effect on people. And normally, I might rage over such a sight. But seeing the two of them—two people I'm utterly obsessed with—clinging together as they worry over me, I've never been happier.

"Come here," I order to Bethany.

She meekly drops her eyes from Viktor's and crawls over the bed, coming to rest next to me.

"You're badly hurt, but you will heal with rest," Viktor informs me, his eyes flittering between Bethany and me. He saved me. I knew he would. I reach forward and take his hand, pulling him to sit. Clutching them both, I breathe easier, relief washing through me.

We're okay.
We're okay.
We're okay.

"And Jessica?" I ask.

Viktor grins wickedly and glances over at Bethany. "She met her end by the hand of your beautiful doll." His amber eyes glimmer with pride, or is it something more? Lust and desire, perhaps. A bittersweet taste fills my mouth. The thought of the two of them naked, at my mercy, has my cock aching with need. "It was poetic and mesmerizing to witness," he says, his voice reverent.

I'm glad Jess is dead. Although, it would have been nice to partake in her suffering. My doll took a life, and I wasn't even conscious to witness it.

Viktor speaks as if he can read the thoughts in my mind. "I will describe it for you later, Monster. Every bloody detail." My heart hammers in my chest. I look forward to hearing that one over again.

"How long have I been out?" I ask, noticing all the bandages covering me and the ones on Bethany's chest.

"Just one day, but your ankle is badly sprained and you lost a lot of blood. You need rest," Viktor says, almost as though he's trying to placate me.

"Show me your wounds," I demand of Bethany.

She gets to her knees and drops the shoulder of her dress down her arms. It pools around her waist and her tits sit there in all their perfect glory. I wait for the urge to cover her and demand Viktor leaves to come over me, but it doesn't. My heart thunders like a hurricane touching down inside my veins.

The idea of him watching her, but not being able to touch her—to know she's within reaching distance but he must remain where he is and just watch as I admire my doll—is a turn on. I want to squeeze her tits while he strokes my cock. Thoughts of Jess touching me the way she did invades the pleasure, and I turn my eyes from Bethany's tits to Viktor's eyes. His gaze is solely on me, fires of need raging in his eyes.

"I had the doctor take blood and swabs," he says, his voice calm. "All my staff had medical evaluations every three months, as you know. I can't risk anything spreading in the club. Hers were clean, and I doubt anything has changed since her last test."

I don't know why I'm even thinking of this shit. I've shared fluids with plenty of people and played in their blood. It's never even been a blip in my mind until…

"It's because you have reason to care now," he answers the question I was asking myself, once again, being more inside my head than I am.

Exhaustion washes over me and my eyelids flutter like lead is being poured over the lashes, dragging them down.

"It's okay. Sleep now. Rest." His words take me under, and I feel the weight of both him and Bethany lift from the bed.

CHAPTER EIGHTEEN

~ Busted ~

Dillon

Waking up on the concrete outside the partially burned down roller rink with a rookie uniform smartass asking me why I was napping on the job is going on the list of reasons I want to fucking put Harris away for the rest of his miserable life. Going inside to see the mess he left beyond the fire he tried to start to get rid of the evidence is also going on the list of fuck yous that motherfucker will be receiving from me when I get back the fingerprints on the murder weapon.

A roller skate.

I thought I'd seen it all with Benny, but no, this new fucker is just as fucked up, if not more so. At least Benny wears his crazy on the outside. Harris wears a cool, untouchable demeanor, but I'm close, and I will take him down.

Jacob found out everything I already knew. Cassian Harris is an alias-forged citizenship. In fact, he forged fucking everything. He does not exist, and the minimum I can get him on now is fraud. If he has Benny back with him, I'll get him too, and put them both where they belong. Then, I can get Elizabeth the help she needs.

"Reeves," I call over.

"Yes, sir?"

"Get this warrant down to Judge Morgan and call me as soon as it's done."

"Yes, sir."

All that is left to do now is find out who the fuck Harris really is. A lot of work went into making him someone new. Russian Viktor is all I've got.

Swiping the box of donuts from Reeves's desk, I make my way back to the hospital.

Jade is up on her feet when I arrive, and it warms my soul to see her doing so well. Her bleeding on the precinct floor was scary as fuck and shaved years from my life.

"Where are Marcus and Elise?" I blurt out, anger flitting through me when I realize they aren't here keeping watch over her.

"Hello to you too," she quips, placing the jug of water she was pouring into a cup down and coming around the bed to curl herself into my arms.

I kiss her beautiful mouth.

"Mmmm, you brought goodies?" She takes the box of donuts, then pouts when she opens it to find only a couple of jam-filled ones left.

"Baby," I growl in irritation. "Seriously, where are Marcus and Elise? I told them not to leave the hospital."

She inspects my appearance and sniffs me. "Elise wanted to change clothes and grab a quick shower, so she went to get them both some fresh items. When was the last time *you* showered?"

"And Marcus?" I demand, ignoring her question. I'm already dialing Elise's number. A ringing sounds out into the room, and Elise's cell phone lights up from the sofa.

Fuck.

"Marcus got a call and left," she says, frowning. "He said he would be right back. Is everything okay?"

"How long ago?" I demand.

She places a hand over her heart, her face paling. "What the hell is going on, Dillon?"

My cell phone lights up, and I recognize it as the number Harris called me from yesterday. "I have to take this. I don't want you leaving this room, Jade. Promise me, no matter what."

Mason begins fussing from the crib in the room. My heart aches to pull him into my arms and soothe him. Unfortunately, I have bigger shit to deal with.

"You're scaring me," she says as she plucks him from the bed and snuggles him against her chest.

"I know. I'm sorry, baby," I reply softly, pressing a quick kiss to her forehead, then to my son's dark head. "Promise me?"

She swallows and nods. "I promise."

Bolting from the room, I answer with a snarl. "You motherfucker. Your time is numbered, Harris, or whatever the fuck your name is. Murder, you can't get out of that one."

His loud chuckle sends chills up my spine. That son of a bitch is scary because of his insanity.

"I have the murder weapon," I snap. "You fucked up when you left it there, probably in a hurry to get Benny out of there."

He makes a sound of disproval. "I think guessing is where you so often go wrong, Detective, and I use that term loosely when referring to you. It's not *my* fingerprints you'll get back from the roller skate."

What?

Benny?

"So, another body to add to Benny's tally. Well, I'll be taking you both in, so be fucking ready."

He chuckles once more. "I'm always ready, and Benny wasn't in any state to leave his prints on the murder weapon, let alone use it." His tone is dark and deadly.

I eventually make it to the parking lot outside the hospital, my frustration reaching an all-time high. "Stop playing games. It has to be one of you."

"You're right there, Detective. You get the best answer by process of elimination. What do they teach you fuckwits at police school anyway?"

My mind races. "There was only you, me, and Elizabeth…"

"Ding. Ding. Ding," he mocks. "We have ourselves a winner."

No.

"You're lying. She couldn't." I saw the body. Face bashed in. Bones crushed. It was barely recognizable. Elizabeth doesn't possess that strength. Or that level of madness.

"Oh, but she could, and she did. It was perfection, Dillon. You should have seen her eyes ignite and the pure elation on her face as she smashed and smashed that cunt. The monster within her was christened with her first taste of blood."

Jesus Christ!

I want to throw my phone and let it shatter into a million pieces. I lost her. She's gone. She's one of them.

"I'm going to end you," I threaten, my voice barely a whisper.

"Well, until then," he says, "I'm going to be needing your help."

A laugh bellows from my chest. This fool is crazier than I thought if he thinks I'm going to do anything for him.

"I have someone on my payroll who can visit your wifey, Dillon. Someone who can inject her with medicine that, instead of heals, kills."

"Threaten her all you like, motherfucker, but no one is getting to her."

"Marcus is a great runner up. How close are you two? As close as Benjamin and me? Like brothers?"

My stomach bottoms out.

"You're lying," I growl.

"What do you want me to do to prove you're wrong? How about I give him matching bullet wounds?"

"Don't do it, Dillon," Marcus shouts in the background. My head is about to explode into flames. Harris has him. He has my fucking partner.

This has to end.

"What do you want?"

"I want you to meet me. There's an alleyway left of the Union Bank, ten minutes from the hospital. Meet me there. Ten minutes is all you get. You fuck me trying to bring backup, I'll bleed Marcus out and make your family my sole mission in life."

He hangs up, and I stew as I jog the half mile to the location near the hospital. I'm panting and out of fucking breath when I round the corner, but draw my Glock, ready to shoot the fuck out of him if necessary.

Elizabeth stands beside Harris, her arms casually hugging his middle, as if he's her favorite damn person in the world. She's tiny and fragile looking compared to the monster in a three-piece suit.

"Where the fuck is he?" I demand.

"He's safe with Benjamin."

You got to be fucking kidding me.

It means he's close, though. In the time it took me to run over here, he and Elizabeth drove from wherever they left Marcus with Benny. Hope is not lost.

"You have my word he will be released," he replies, his jaw clenching. "As soon as I have Kami."

Kami again.

I can't give her to him.

"I'm going in there to get her with or without your help," he snaps, his mask of coolness gone as rage takes over. "Without it, a lot of people die, including your wife and baby."

I'm wondering how quickly I can pull off a shot and kill this motherfucker. "Why is Kami so important to you?" I demand, hoping to distract him from thoughts of murdering my family.

Elizabeth looks up at him at my question, her cheeks turning pink.

"Are you going to help or not?" he seethes, ignoring me altogether.

"Fine."

He motions for me to hand over my gun. I slap it in his hand, and he winks. "In you go, sweetheart." Then, he makes a loud sniffing sound. "They call them baths, Detective. You should consider taking one."

How the fuck I keep ending up in the back of his car is infuriating, and Marcus getting himself caught is going to get him an ass beating by me once I get him back.

"Marcus was easy to lure," Harris croons, as if he's inside my motherfucking head. "He has quite a thing for Elise. She does nothing for me. I don't see the appeal."

"Because you prefer your partners a little more insane," I growl.

"No, Detective, a little more free." He stares over at Elizabeth, and she bites her lip.

I fucking hate this guy.

He slams the butt of my gun across my skull, and I'm forced into a much-needed nap.

CHAPTER NINETEEN

~ Collapsed ~

Viktor

It was such a relief to see those dark eyes of my monster staring into my soul. All the words he wanted to say were conveyed right there for me to read in his touch and gaze.

He realizes now what we are together.

I need to get Kami back and stem the bleeding of my entire world. If Dillon finds out who I am and any of this gets back to my father, he will also feel the need to do some damage control. I absolutely do not want my father cleaning up another one of my life's messes.

My mind flits to my doll, then my monster.

They're both perfect in every sense.

I can't live without them, and I refuse to. I was condemned and sent away when my father learned who I was. He stripped me of my name and told me the world—his world—would believe I died in The V Games. That Niko's death would become my own. That it happened so close to the exit, it wasn't seen by the spectators.

Vlad insisted, though, that I was sent to America, like I always dreamed of, and wired money to me to get myself up and running. He told me to build my own empire and show our father he made a mistake. That when my kingdom was big enough, Father would call upon me to rejoin our family.

I miss my family, but I have a new one now, and they are what I need.

As we drive with our prisoner in tow, I think back to earlier when I'd received a text.

Luke: The monitor you had me install at the Stanton house when I grabbed clothes just lit up. Elise is home.

I'd had him get me Marcus James's cell number. The cop was easy to lure, and his mouth opened and rattled out everything I wanted to know. He really loves Elise and doesn't have a clue that I didn't really take her or that she left her house and I allowed her to do so. The threat of me having her was enough to have him come running.

Elizabeth squeezes my hand across the console of the vehicle. I pull it into my lap against my cock that hasn't seemed to settle now that I have both her and Benjamin back. A soft gasp escapes her, but she doesn't pull away. My mind drifts to earlier before we came for Dillon.

"So, my mother is taking care of Kami and Jade," Elizabeth breathes.

"Why are you here with him?" Marcus spits out. "We've been going crazy looking for you. Elise is out of her mind with worry."

Elizabeth rolls her eyes at Marcus's outrage. "My dear sister only cares about herself, trust me. You will find that out the hard way. We all do."

"You're fucking crazy, just like your daddy," he barks out.

I slap a strip of tape over his mouth to shut him up.

"You're nothing like him," I assure her, cupping her chin in my hands and offering a chaste kiss to her lips. "You're like Monster." I gesture to his sleeping form, a beast at peace. "Perfect in every way."

Her face blooms pink and she bats her lashes as she looks up at me, transfixed.

"I can help you," she murmurs. "To distract my mother while you get to Kami."

"See, perfect." I repeat. "Let's do this."

Elizabeth squeezes my hand again, and I drag my mind from my thoughts, stealing a glance at her. Her plump bottom lip is caught between her teeth as she rubs her thighs together.

I'm going to fuck this doll very soon.

And my monster will learn to be okay with it.

CHAPTER TWENTY

~ Separated ~

Elizabeth

"I'm scared," I admit, my voice ragged. I'm starving and tired and sad. Will Kami change things for us? I'm growing fond of Viktor's presence.

Viktor releases my hand to reach over and squeeze my thigh just below the hem of my dress. Soon, we'll head back over to the hospital. Currents of need ripple through me. I squirm at his touch, unsure whether I want it or not, but he doesn't move his hand away. Instead, he begins stroking my flesh. It dizzies and confuses me. I belong to Benny, yet here I want to spread my legs open to let him touch me.

Shame courses through me.

"He felt the same way," Viktor murmurs, his fingertips grazing along the seam of my panties under my dress. "He only had eyes for you. But he knew deep down there was something between us. He hated Kami because she had what he wanted."

Tears well in my eyes, and I let out a choked sound. "You...she had you?"

"Yes," he says softly as his finger dips below the fabric

and touches the lip of my pussy, causing me to whimper. "Benny and I, we're…"

They're what?

Together?

Betrayal knifes its way through me, but then my eyes flutter closed. Viktor is teasing my clit and images of him and Benny naked, rolling around in his bed, have me panting. I smelled sex in the air when he'd taken me to his home. Deep down, I knew what they'd done. But who fucked who? Did Benny overpower Viktor and take him in the ass? My pussy clenches at that thought.

The car suddenly comes to a stop as he pulls into a mostly empty parking garage. "Where does that leave me?" I choke out, sorrow saturating my chest and drowning me. If they don't want me, what will I do?

"Come here," Viktor growls. He slips his hand from my panties before dragging me into his lap to straddle him. I whimper at feeling his hardness pressed against me. He caresses my throat with his hand before tilting my head up so he can look at me. "Benny and I have something impenetrable. Solid. Powerful."

I burst into tears. I can see the truth in his eyes. "And what do we have, he and I? What about you and I? Where will that leave me?"

Hot lips press to mine as his palms slide to my ass. He uses my body to grind against his length through his slacks. Pleasure zings through me.

"It leaves you right in the middle," he breathes against my mouth. "Benny loves you, and I love him. We're a family now."

His words seem too good to be true.

"What about Kami? Was she your family too?" Dillon snarls from the back. Someone has woken up.

Viktor stiffens and pulls away from my mouth. The loss is hollowing. I want his lips back on mine. Reassuring me. Telling me promises that seem too good to be true.

"Kami has nothing to do with *this*," Viktor snaps, pointing his finger between the two of us. But then he's calm again as his hands slide under my dress. He moves one hand to my front, and pushes my panties to the side. The moment his finger enters me, I moan. His thumb rubs against my clit, and I shamelessly work my hips in cadence with his touch.

"You're sick, Elizabeth," Dillon whispers from the back, as if I disgust him. "You need help."

I start to pout, but Viktor devours my mouth. "You're not sick, sweet doll," Viktor coos. "You're perfect. Benjamin thinks so, and I do too." His words are a salve to my heart. My pussy throbs with need.

"Do you want to be inside me, Viktor?" I ask, but it's more a plea.

"Shhh," he murmurs, his teeth nipping at my lip. "You'll have everything you could ever wish for soon. But we aren't taking that step without him. He'll want to be in charge. You know how our monster is."

I do.

He's a beast and wild, but he likes to be in control.

"Stop touching her, motherfucker!" Dillon roars from the back. He kicks at the window several times, but it doesn't break.

"Come for me, doll," Viktor urges, his voice breathy. "Come all over my finger. Benjamin would want that.

When we get home to him, I will let him suck you right off my finger. Do you want that, you perfect little doll?"

I nod and tilt my head back. His lips find the cut on my throat Benny had inflicted. He's gentle and soothing as he licks away the pain there while his finger works me from the inside. I'm desperate to touch him and unbuckle his belt. He groans when I unzip his slacks and pull out his cock.

"We can't," he warns, his voice hard, sending shivers through me.

"But—"

"No, bad doll," he chides. "He wouldn't like it."

"*I* don't fucking like it. You sick fucks." Dillon struggles and groans.

But I ignore him. This is just like my site. He's just a viewer in my private world.

I stroke Viktor's length and pretend he's inside me. Will Benny be happy? Will he want to share me with his lover? I don't know how the dynamics will work, but I'm so starved by the idea of it, my stomach growls.

Viktor chuckles against my collarbone before nipping my flesh there. "I'll feed you as soon as Benjamin allows it." But he's not rushing to get me off. It's as though he enjoys teasing me.

I can tease too.

Running my thumb over the tip of his cock, I revel in how it seeps at the top. "Will you both put your cocks in me at once?" I ask, my question so soft, he probably feels it more than he hears it. Dillon is too busy growling and kicking the windows to notice.

"If it pleases him," he groans.

"What about what pleases me?"

"He's claimed us both, don't you see? We're here to make him happy. And you'll both make me happy."

For a brief moment, I wonder if I'm being played, but then he's kissing my mouth again with reverence. It's real. I can almost taste his love for Benny on his tongue. I know the taste.

He jerks his finger from inside me so he can cradle my face as he kisses me. I need his touch, so I shamelessly rub against his shaft with my pussy, keeping my panties pulled to the side beneath my dress so I can feel his skin against mine. Our grunts and groans are purely animalistic. When the tip of his cock pokes my entrance, I whimper. Bucking his hips hard, he penetrates me deep, and I scream loud enough to wake the dead.

"Fuck, that was an accident," he groans as he grips my hips and pulls me off. But he doesn't let me go and uses my body to rub my pussy along his now-soaked cock. I'm buzzing with a thousand emotions and sensations.

I'm dying.

I'm living.

Oh, shit, I'm coming.

Stars glitter around me as my screams pierce the air. Viktor bites on my chin and grunts a second before wet heat splatters my lower stomach. His cock slips and pushes inside me again, causing us both to moan, but then he pulls me back off him. I'm crushed against his chest and he kisses my ear.

"We're a family now," he murmurs, his hot breath tickling me.

I cling to him as he strokes my hair.

"Now, get buckled up. I'm in charge of keeping you safe while he's recouping."

I reluctantly pull from his grip, but I'm anxious to get back to our monster. Once I'm settled in my seat, he reaches over me and buckles me in, then winks at me before putting the vehicle into drive again.

We ignore the snarling from the back as we go to get Kami back for him.

CHAPTER TWENTY-ONE

~ Crippled ~

Viktor

Everything seems as though it's coming together. With Benjamin home and Detective Dipshit in the backseat of my SUV, we will get Kami back and my identity will be safe.

Dillon was enraged when I took Monster's doll in my arms and she straddled my lap while I pleasured her. The sounds of fury coming from the back were almost comical while she panted and moaned, pleading for me to make her feel good.

Now, he won't speak to me or sweet Elizabeth. Probably better that way. She clings to my hand across the console of the vehicle as though I have the power to protect her. And I do. I will. For Benjamin. For me. For her.

We pull up at the hospital around the back where Dillon told me to go.

"I'm going to take those cuffs off, Detective," I tell him simply. "But if you try any shit, I'll slit the throats of everyone you know."

"Got it," he snaps.

I climb out of the vehicle and open the door. Elizabeth

does the honors of unlocking the cuffs. He gapes at me when I hand him his gun back. Mine stays trained on him.

"You're stupid if you don't think I'll use this gun on you," Dillon barks, pointing his weapon at me.

"Tell him," I say to Elizabeth, unfazed.

"We have Elise, as well as Marcus, and Benny didn't get the satisfaction of killing Jessica, so he's hungry to feed his demons." She smooths her hair with her fingers and shrugs. "If he doesn't make the call to let Benny know you're playing ball, I become sister-less and you lose a partner." Her lip trembles, but it's all for a fucking show. Cutest little faker I've ever seen. "And I don't know what will happen to Jade and MJ."

I smile. "I do. They die."

Dillon's jaw clenches, but he nods, his gun lowering.

"Let's go," I grunt, stalking for the side of the building.

ABillon is smarter than he looks, because he walks after me, his attention alert. Elizabeth hurries up behind me and clings to my jacket. It would be so easy for Dillon to pluck her from me, put a bullet in my skull, and leave.

But I guess he cares for that little partner of his. And at this point, he surely knows our doll would fight him before she let anything happen to Benny or me.

"We need to put our weapons away while we go inside," he utters. "I have officers at the doors and don't want them to get suspicious."

And I agree. We both harness our weapons, and my heart thuds with every step we take in their direction.

"Sir." Two uniformed officers tip their head in greeting.

"I will take it from here," he barks in an authoritative

manner. "Go take a break."

They look at each other and smile. "Yes, sir."

Dillon punches in a code, and the door gives beneath his palm. A doctor I recognize as our little doll's mother lifts her head at our presence, and her mouth drops.

"Elizabeth," she cries out, running around the counter and rushing to her daughter before collecting her up in her arms.

I've already taken my gun back out and am nudging Dillon to move forward. "Where is she?"

"The last room." He nods his head to signal a door at the end of the corridor.

I take a step toward it, passing another door. The window shows Jade inside—and Elise. Well, shit.

I'm already at Kami's door when Dillon notices Elise is very much safe. An error on my part. I push open Kami's door and her eyes lift to find mine as I storm in.

"I'm sorry," she meekly tells me, and my stomach knots with betrayal.

Has she told Dillon who I am?

She wouldn't.

She fucking wouldn't.

"Put the gun down," Dillon orders, pointing his own at me.

"We still have Marcus," I remind him through clenched teeth.

He nods his head. "Yes, but I can't let you take Kami from here. Marcus wouldn't want me to, and I won't."

I flash my eyes to Elizabeth, who launches herself toward Dillon. Unfortunately, her mother restrains her and sticks a needle in her arm. Her eyes blaze and dart to mine to save her, but whatever the fuck it is her mother drugged her with takes full effect and her eyes droop. Her body becomes limp, causing her mother to lower her to the floor.

"If you shoot me, I can't make the call and Marcus dies," I growl. "Benny *will* kill him."

"Benny is dead," Kami pipes up, her bottom lip trembling.

My eyes drag back to her. "What?"

"I'm sorry, Viktor, but Vlad is here." A weak tear leaks from her eye. "He came for Benny."

She. Fucking. Betrayed. Me.

My reactions are organic, not thought through at all, and my arm moves from Dillon to her. With one shot, I put a bullet straight through her traitorous skull.

Dead.

Dead.

Dead.

I ended Kami, a giant piece of my fucking heart, and I didn't think twice. It didn't hurt. I felt nothing.

But the moment she admitted to betraying me and that Benny was as good as dead, I'd felt that pain to my motherfucking soul. Crushing. Hollowing. Fucking insane. There's no doubt. If Vlad is here, Benjamin will die if he isn't already bled out all over my bed, gasping his last breaths without me. My brother moves like the night. He's darkness and stealth. No hesitation. If Kami told him he was a weakness to me, Vlad would have eliminated said weakness.

Now, as I sit in the back of a cruiser on the way to the

police station, I have only one thought.

Elizabeth.

She needs me.

She needs me to get my shit together and free her from those maggots.

I'll take her away with me. We'll run far from here and mourn our loss together. When I was inside her, for those two brief moments, I'd felt whole. Between Benjamin and Elizabeth, I'd finally felt filled with something I'd been searching for my entire life. I was no longer hollow. I was complete.

As quickly as it was given to me, it was taken away.

Ripped to goddamn shreds.

Fuck.

I ignore Dillon's smug taunting from the driver's seat. Instead, I grit my teeth and find the will to calm myself. I'm not unmasked rage. I am in control.

Breathe, Viktor.

Find your fucking balance.

I close my eyes and think of the way it felt when Benjamin's mouth was on mine. How he drove into me as though he thought it could punish me. His feelings poured from him, and I drank every single one of them up. Lust. Love. Confusion. I wanted to sip slowly and revel in the taste, but I'm a greedy fuck. I gulped from him. I'm still drunk from how he made me feel.

It was enough.

More than enough.

But then I had that tiny doll in my arms and the sensations were overwhelming again. Is it because they're siblings? I'm so greedy I need them both? The moment she clung to me that first time, I knew. With him loving her so much, and me loving him, it would have to work. Three of us. A trio. A motherfucking family unit.

All that was solidified the moment I had my finger inside her. Her body was sweet perfection, and she freely shared it with me. The need rippling from her was desperate. As though she wanted to consume me. The monstrous villain that lives behind her pretty wide doll eyes is the same one that lives within Benjamin and me.

Lived.

His monster is most likely gutted like a pig for slaughter if I know my brother.

An ache settles in my chest but the thought of her seems to soothe it. If he is dead, then she's all I have left. I'll do anything to have her back in my arms.

My cock thickens as I remember how it felt to push inside her tight pussy. Choked my dick to the point I thought I'd come immediately. The idea of shooting my seed deep inside her nearly makes me manic.

Would Monster have allowed it?

Perhaps if I sucked his cock at the same time, he might have felt more than giving.

Images of the three of us tangled up in a messy, fucked-up, evil scene is gratifying. It ignites the fires within me. Gives me motherfucking hope. I'll find a way to get out of this shitshow Detective Dickface has put me in and I'll get my family back. Kami could have been lying. Benny could still be alive.

I was sent away from a family once before.

I'll be damned if I let that happen again.

"Out you go, psycho." Dillon jerks on my bicep, and I

realize we're at the precinct already. He guides me into the building, his smug satisfaction practically rippling from him in waves.

I'll end everyone he loves the moment I get my chance.

Everyone but Elizabeth, of course.

She. Is. Ours.

Our precious little monstrous doll.

He guides me past some rooms labeled *Interrogation* and into the holding area. I pass tatted-up criminals and gangsters. Dumb fucks who actually belong in such a scuzzy place.

I'm trapped in my thoughts as I go through the motions of getting booked. Under Cassian Harris, of course. That's all they can do. For now. Until they uncover who I really am, thanks to that traitorous cunt Kami.

Instead of hurting, I erect walls.

Just like when Vika betrayed me.

My sister. My sweet sister. She ruined me.

Kami ruined me too.

They may think they can take me out of the game, but little do they realize, I'm the master.

I just make up new rules.

I always fucking win.

CHAPTER TWENTY-TWO

~ Crumbled ~

Benny

"Dillon won't allow you to manipulate him," Marcus says from the chair he's been tied to.

I sit up and stretch. Everything fucking hurts, but I'm feeling better. I don't think my ankle is broken, just a sprain and already healing well enough for me to put my weight on it. The cuts pull tight on my skin, but it's nothing compared to the burns I sustained thanks to Dillon years ago. I have a high threshold for pain, and the battlefield is where I long to sustain that high. Fuck Dillon and fuck Jessica. They only make me stronger.

"Shut up," I snap. It's been two days since they left with a note on my bedside. They went to retrieve Kami—the stupid whore—much to my fury, but never succeeded. I've been watching the news to plan out my next move. From what I can tell, Elizabeth, "the kidnapping victim," is being held at the hospital for observations, and Cassian Harris is being held for the murder of a woman whose identity they don't really know yet.

They keep showing pictures of Kami, and each time, I break out into a motherfucking grin. He did it. He truly did it. Ended that cunt's life like he should have years ago.

For me.

I'm dying to walk into that hospital, blow shit up, and take my perfect doll home. But if Viktor taught me anything, it's to be patient. We're playing a game. All moves must be thought through and analyzed. I can rest assured Viktor is sitting in that cell formulating the biggest move of all.

"You may as well let me go. Then, maybe you can just fucking leave. If you stay, Dillon will find you. He was on to Harris. It'll only be a matter of time before they discover the location of his home," Marcus says, his eyes manic. Starving for two days will do that to a man. "They're coming for you, Benny. You better run, run, run before it's too late."

I slap at the side of my head to get him out of there. The only person I've felt comfortable with intruding is Viktor. Fuck, I need him back. He always knows what to do.

"Your bullshit cop tactics don't work on me," I snarl. "In fact, I think I'm tired of hearing your mouth. Maybe I should cut out your tongue and send it to Dillon. Tell him I'll do the same to his wife if he doesn't cooperate."

The plan feels like the most solid one I've had. I stand from the bed and limp over to Marcus. His eyes widen when I unsheathe my knife from my belt. Blood is encrusted near the hilt. It's ended so many lives, I'm not sure whose blood it is at this point. One thing's for sure, though: it'll be Marcus's soon.

"I gotta know something, man," he grits out. "Before you hack me to pieces. Why'd you stop caring?"

I tense and growl. "What?"

"About Jade? I've read the criminal profile on you. The shit you did to her. You were fucking obsessed. A psychopath dead set on keeping his prize. Then you discarded her. Like you didn't care anymore. Are you that mental?"

I grip the front of his dress shirt and yank him closer, digging the knife slightly into his throat. "I'm not someone you can profile, goddammit. I don't follow your cop rules, asshole. I make my own. This is my world."

He laughs. "He played you, man. Harris got inside your head and played you. You're in this predicament because it's actually *his* world. You're nothing but a pawn, man."

I'm so enraged, my only thought is slicing this cop to bits. I don't need him. In fact, he's slowing me down. I need to leave this house and find a way to force Dillon to give me what I want. Marcus thinks I forgot about Jade? The asshole doesn't know me at all. I'll remember exactly the way her ass feels when I'm ramming the barrel of my gun inside of it. I bet it'll only take three seconds of that shit for Dillon to make some motherfucking miracles happen. I didn't just discard her. She was everything, but she was a temporary fix for a deep-rooted need, and once Bethany came back to me, I didn't need my dirty doll anymore. She became the past—a filler until I was reunited with Bethany. A good filler. Revisiting past pleasures to further our agenda won't be such a chore.

"I wouldn't do that if I were you," a smooth, deep, calm voice resounds from behind me.

Familiar. Thick. Accented.

Viktor?

I jerk away from Marcus and gape when I see someone who could be his twin.

"Who the fuck are you?" I demand, my hand tightening on the blade.

The man stands a few inches taller than Viktor and a bit wider. His dark, almost black, hair is styled similar to Viktor's, but a few strands of grey at his temples depicts he's definitely a bit older.

"I am Vlad Vasiliev. Viktor's older brother." He lifts a black eyebrow. "You must be Benjamin Stanton. His lover, no?"

Fuck, he sounds just like Viktor, aside for the more prominent Russian accent, and it's messing with my head. The same deep timbre that rattles its way straight to my cock is there.

"What do you want?" I may trust Viktor, but I don't trust this smug asshole, and Viktor always froze up when mentioning his past. It's a painful subject for him. Why is this brother here in our world telling me what to fucking do?

Marcus snorts from behind me. "Lover? No wonder you weren't interested in Jade anymore."

Vlad's brows furrow together. "When you starve or torture your victim, they tend to lose their minds a bit. How long has this one been under your care, Benjamin?"

I grit my teeth. I fucking hate how he seems to know my situation and uses my name like we're acquaintances. "What. Do. You. Want?" I don't ask how the fuck he got in here.

Vlad lets out a sigh and pulls his hands from his pockets. I fixate on the leather gloves. He cracks each knuckle slowly, then cracks his neck before fixating his blazing amber eyes on mine.

"Your head."

Marcus starts cackling. Okay, so starving the motherfucker has made him go a little crazy.

I hold my knife out in front of me. He can fucking try. I'll have his throat flayed open before he can even come around the side of the bed.

Vlad smiles at me, brilliant and charming. "Well, it *was* what I wanted. But now, witnessing things for myself, I realize my original intentions may need to be reevaluated."

So, he talks in riddles like his brother.

This family is something else.

"Viktor doesn't take kindly to betrayal," I bite out. "You should ask your sister." I don't know the whole story, but seeing his slight flinch satisfies me, knowing my words hit their intended mark.

"I'm not going to kill you, Benjamin. I'm going to help you."

My hackles rise when he pulls a gun out from inside his fancy-ass suit jacket and begins screwing a suppressor on the end. Marcus continues to laugh like a goddamn lunatic from his chair.

"He's going to help you, all right," Marcus snorts.

I don't have time to react. One moment, Vlad is fiddling with his gun, and the next, lightning quick, he has it raised and pointed at me. He fires the weapon, but with the silencer, all it makes is a *pfft* sound.

Stunned, I wait for the bullet to impact.

Instead, I hear glass breaking.

Shouts resound outside the window, and I hear

cracking within the house. It makes sense for Vlad to know where his brother lives, but no one else knows. Detective Dipshit couldn't have figured it out this quickly, could he?

Vlad moves like a lethal cat and swoops his arm around as someone blasts through the door behind him. The bullet pierces the man's skull. Another man charges in and manages to swat the gun from Vlad's grip. Before I can move to assist, Vlad pulls a knife from his belt.

With movements that remind me of Viktor, he effortlessly punches the knife into the man's torso countless times. The man groans and slumps to the floor.

"Wait!" a voice shouts from within the house.

Vlad bends to pick up the gun and shoots me a glare. "Don't say a word." Then, he hollers out of the bedroom. "Bring him in."

I can't help but grin like the cat that ate the canary when Dillon walks into the room, both hands above his head.

"You killed my men," he spits out at Vlad.

"Should have brought more than six," Vlad replies, his features relaxed, as if he didn't just end three men within seconds. "I trust my men did their jobs out there?"

Dillon's face turns purple with rage. "Who the fuck are you?"

A giant man in a suit stands behind Dillon with an assault rifle pressed into his back.

Vlad walks over to him and smiles. "I think you know. In fact, I'm pretty sure Klara used your phone to call me."

"So why isn't he dead yet?" Dillon roars, his hate-filled glare burning holes through me.

"Because they're making deals, D." Crazy-ass Marcus

is thinking clearly now. Dumb fuck.

"Yes," Vlad agrees. "We are. And it's time you enter the negotiations, Detective. I've done a little research. The plane ride from my homeland was achingly long and boring. I know everything about you. Down to the fact that you named your son Mason. Mason and sweet Jade are doing well now that they're settled in back at home. How's MJ handling the new baby? Is she a good big sister? Do the cops you have watching the house not frighten her?"

Dillon's rage simmers. "What do you want?"

"I want Viktor. You're to release him and let us go on our merry little way. Your nightmare ends today, Detective. Aren't you exhausted? I know you have a new baby and all, but the bags under your eyes say you've been working too hard."

I want to rush over and push my blade into Dillon's fucking heart, but I'm not a psychopath like Marcus claims. I'm smarter. A well-trained monster. A master of his own game.

Control.

I wield it like a weapon—a weapon Viktor taught me to use. If I kill him, we can't get him to free Viktor.

"You know I can't do that," Dillon growls, but his voice has lost some bite.

"Can't or won't? Because either way, I get what I want—with or without your assistance. I know people, Detective. Yes, they may take their time, but I will get what I want. But by defying me, you'll lose. This game will be all over for you. Over for Mason. Over for MJ. Over for Jade." Vlad darts his gaze over to me and glances at Marcus. "Over for Elise and Elizabeth too."

My blood boils, but it's snuffed out when Vlad shoots me a look of reassurance. It's one I've come to trust from his brother. His threats are for Dillon, not me.

"Fuck!" Dillon rages. "You killed my men! How do I know I can trust you?"

Vlad steps forward, narrowing his eyes. "I didn't kill that one." He points to Marcus. "Benjamin is going to leave. Then, you and I are going to walk into that police station with Viktor's lawyer. We'll hide out in the interrogation room for a bit, then we'll walk out. You'll tell them he's posted bail or whatever the fuck you have to say to get my brother out of there."

"No!" Dillon yells. "Fuck no!"

Vlad smiles, but it's cold and deadly. His mask falters for a moment, and I get a glimpse of his monster. "Listen clearly. This isn't a question. It's a statement. You will do this. And then I, to show good faith, will take my brother away. You'll never see or hear from him again."

"And him?" Dillon glares at me, hate brimming in his eyes.

"If he is a friend of Viktor's, then he is a friend of mine. Which means, he also goes away." Vlad taps the end of his silencer on Dillon's nose. "It means your partner lives and your problems disappear. Jade can rest easy at night. Maybe pop out a few more children before you die of a damn heart attack."

"Just that simple?" Dillon asks, astonished. "You take these fuckers away and my life goes back to normal?"

"It will be that simple. If you allow it to be. But if you go fucking shit up and complicating manners, I will be forced to change the game. Is that what you want? For me to have a reason to end your pretty little family?" Vlad asks, venom dripping from his tone. "Trust me when I tell you, you are nothing. You will be replaced by another detective who has a precious family he wants to keep safe. It's only that I want Viktor sooner rather than later that I'm allowing you to still breathe. Do we deal with you or the next detective who takes your place when I kill you?"

Dillon bows his head, his shouldering trembling with anger.

"You have to do it, D," Marcus utters from beside me. "As much as I fucking hate this, it needs to be done. We have families."

Dillon meets his gaze, and understanding passes between them. It's then that I realize they've left out a very important part of the negotiations. *My doll.* When I open my mouth, Vlad barks at me.

"Benjamin. Wait in the second SUV outside." His eyes implore me to obey, and everything in me screams to go rogue and do my own shit. I fist my hand, wondering if I should.

Family.

Family looks out for one another.

If I can accept Viktor as my family, that means I have to trust one of the few people he loves: his brother. That means this fucker is *my* brother too.

"Got it, boss," I grind out.

Vlad gives me a slight nod of approval.

"See you in your dreams, Detective," I say as I stalk past him.

"We'll meet again in hell," Dillon barks back.

CHAPTER TWENTY-THREE

~ Demolished ~

Elizabeth

The medications make me feel woozy and not like myself. I can't focus. The only time I'm happy is when I'm asleep. When I dream of Monster and Master. The three of us together. Happy.

But then I always wake up.

Clarity finds me and reminds me Benny is gone.

That Viktor is in jail.

My life is over.

"Knock, knock," Mom says as she enters my room. I'm still in the psychiatric ward of the hospital—the place I've been since Viktor shot Kami two days ago.

I try to roll away from her voice, but my arms are restrained. Fire burns through my blood, chasing away the haziness, but I can't escape her.

For two days, Jade, my sister, and my mother have all tried to bring me back to them. I don't belong to them. I never did.

"I'm about to go do my rounds, but I wanted to check on you before bed." She frowns as she swipes my sweaty hair from my forehead. "Oh, baby, you look so tired. Do you want something to help you sleep?"

As much as I don't want to answer her, I do. "Please, Momma. I don't want to be on these meds anymore."

Her features soften. "I know. We'll get you out of this dark place and soon you won't have to. Just keep trying for me, okay?"

The rage explodes within me, but I tamper it down. Going crazy isn't going to help my case. I need her to feel sorry for me.

"My wrists hurt," I lie, forcing fat tears into my eyes.

Mom purses her lips together and her nostrils flare. "Why did you do it?"

I blink at her in confusion, a hot tear leaking down my temple. "Do what?"

"You killed that woman." She makes a choking sound. "With a roller skate. Your prints were all over it. Dillon's doing his best to keep them from pulling you out of here and sending you over to the prison. He wants you to plead insanity. Is that what happened? I just need to know."

I still at her words. Thoughts of Jessica Johnson riding Benny's cock have clouds of red blinding me. I scream and twist in the bed. "THE WHORE DESERVED IT!"

Mom jolts away from me as though she might get burned. "You're just like him. Like your father. Like your brother." A sob escapes her. "I tried so hard. It was never good enough."

My body relaxes, and I spit out, "*I* was never good enough. When you chose Elise over me, I had to find my own family. Someone who understood me and loved me. You sure as hell didn't."

Mom bursts into tears and rushes from the room

without another word. I fight against my restraints to no avail. Eventually, I tire out and cry. My grief is overwhelming. Crushing and consuming.

I'm still crying when a nurse in scrubs walks into the room hours later, pushing a wheelchair, limping slightly. He wears a surgical mask and cap. When his eyes lift to mine, I stop breathing.

I must be dreaming.

This isn't real.

Chocolate brown eyes pin me with a heated stare. Familiar. Filled with love. Mine. My monster.

"Master," I choke out.

He rushes over to me and runs his fingertips along my jaw. "What have they done to you?"

I start to sob when he pulls out a knife. Not because I'm afraid, but because I'm overwhelmed with happiness. He saws through my bindings, only nicking me a little in the process, and frees me. I'm easily hoisted into his strong arms.

"You're alive. I overhead the officers talking. Viktor shot Kami and they said you were dead," I whisper as I clutch his cheeks. Desperately, I pull the mask down and admire his mouth. His beard has been clipped short to a simple scruff. "Kiss me."

Leaning forward, he captures my lips with his. His tongue is strong and assertive as he owns my mouth. I want it all over me. In me. When he breaks away, I whimper.

"We don't have time for this, Doll." His tone is gruff, but I understand. If we plan to escape, I need to help.

"Okay. Let's get out of here."

Once I'm situated in the wheelchair, he pulls his mask

back into place. It's late, so hardly any people are hanging around the psyche ward. With points of my finger, I guide him down the least traveled hallways. We avoid the busier areas, and soon, we're in the back parking lot. He abandons the wheelchair and carries me to a vehicle.

"Get some rest," he says once we're pulling away. "It's a long drive."

I wake up when I hear the sound of gravel beneath the car. Sitting up in my seat, I ignore the pounding headache nearly blinding me. We drive up to a nice home surrounded by trees.

"Where are we?" My voice croaks from sleep and thirst.

"A place Vlad set up."

Vlad?

He shuts off the car, but before he can climb out, I attack. I've missed him so much and knowing he's not dead ignites a thousand fires inside me. I scramble into his lap and straddle him. His groans of need quench my thirst. I want to lap them up.

The ripping of my hospital gown is my only warning before I'm completely naked in his arms. His palms greedily grip at my breasts while I tug at the button of his jeans in desperation. Within seconds, I have his hard cock pulled out and he's torn away his shirt. We both still as we inspect the damage that bitch inflicted.

"You killed her," he mutters, his voice reverent.

"For you," I pant.

Our eyes meet, and his flicker with need. His fingers

bite into my hips, and I crush my lips to his. I grip his cock between us and line it up with my soaked pussy. When I sink down on his length, we both groan. An ache forms in my chest when I realize I had Viktor in this same position just a couple days ago.

A loud sob rips from me.

I miss him.

Benny grips my jaw and angles my head down so he can look into my teary eyes. "We'll get him back. Soon, Doll. And then we'll be whole."

How does he know?

Am I that transparent?

I rock my hips, and his fingers bruise my flesh as he bucks his hips into me. He's thick and it's almost painful, but it's a sweet sort of pain. It makes me feel alive.

"I love you, my pretty little doll," he groans against my mouth. His teeth nip at my bottom lip as his thumb rubs against my clit. Pleasure zings around me, and I fall back against the steering wheel. His eyes are wild and manic as he visually devours me. "Tell me what I need to hear."

I moan when he pinches my clit. An orgasm splits through me and seems to steal my soul straight from my body. I clench around him and cry out as his heat gushes deep inside me. Knowing I'm no longer on the pill makes my heart hammer. He's marking me. I'm his. Forever.

"I love you too, Master," I purr as I sit up and kiss his mouth again.

He tangles his fingers in my hair and pulls me back slightly so he can stare at me. His brown eyes soften as he regards me. "*Monster*. You're not to call me Master anymore."

My brows crash together. "But—"

"*I'm* Monster. *He's* Master." His kisses my mouth. "And *you're* our perfect little doll."

I run my fingers through his hair that's still buzzed short and stare at him in confusion. "You told me you were the master."

"We all have our roles," he mutters, his stare on my mouth. "I'm no longer going to fight them. I won't fight *any* of my urges anymore. You. Him. It's what I want."

"I want it too," I breathe.

His cock jolts back awake inside me.

"I have to tell you something," I squeak out. "I can't start this on lies."

He darts his eyes all over me. "Tell me what?"

"When we went to deal with Kami," I whisper, shame rippling through me, "he and I…"

"You fucked?"

His body is tense. Coiled and ready to spring.

"Not exactly." I lift my gaze to his. "We both were so overwhelmed at having you back. The way he talks about you…with such love…" I bite on my lip, "it turns me on."

He snags my throat in his brutal grip, his eyes wild with mania. "What did you do?"

I choke out my words until he loosens his grip. "He touched me. Made me come. I felt him on me. Inside me." I lick my lips. "It didn't feel right, though. Like we were missing a piece."

"When we get him back," he snarls, his grip once again tightening, "I'm going to take turns putting it in each of your asses."

I moan and rock against him. "You *are* the master."

"No," he growls against my mouth, sucking on my bottom lip hard enough to make my pussy clench in response. "You both are my dolls. I'm your monster. I fucking own you both."

He doesn't come, but instead shoves me over into the passenger seat. I'm just sitting up when my car door flies open. He plucks me from the vehicle and carries my naked body into a house I've never seen before. We barely make it into the kitchen before he has me bent over the table. His cock pushes into my pussy, then he pulls it out. I scream in pain, my fingernails gouging marks into the wood, when the tip of his cock begins proding into my ass. I try to scramble away, but he grabs a handful of my hair and yanks as he drives all the way into me.

The pain is harsh, but beautiful. It kills me, yet it breathes life into me. I hate it, but I love it. He grunts and grunts until he empties his seed deep inside the place he set on fire. He's dragging me to hell with him, and I don't even want to put up a fight. When he pulls out roughly, I nearly vomit from the pain of it. I'm worried I'm bleeding or worse.

"I'm sorry," I sob. "I didn't mean to hurt you. I love you."

He tugs me into his arms, and there isn't anger shining in his eyes. No, his browns swirl like melted chocolate. He grins at me, and I'm positive it's the most beautiful thing I've ever seen.

"You didn't hurt me, Doll." His lips crash to mine. "When you talk about him," he breathes against my mouth, "it just really turns me on. You free the beast."

Eager to lure the monster even further from the cage,

I narrow my eyes. "His cock was in me twice. I wanted him to come inside me."

The growl that roars from him is downright terrifying. He tosses me on the hard surface of the table before roughly flipping me back onto my stomach. I'm worried he'll take my ass again when fire cracks against my flesh.

Whap!

Whap!

Whap!

He whips my ass with his strong hand until I'm not sure I'll be able to sit. I cry and don't have the strength to move.

"Do you like it when I beat your ass for taunting me?" he hisses, his palm soothing away the sting.

"Do you like it when I talk about Viktor and I fucking around without you?" I challenge back, twisting my head to look up at him.

Provoking my beast is my new favorite thing.

His lust-glazed eyes tell me he likes it a lot.

"I asked him if you'd both put your cocks inside me at once," I murmur. "Will you?"

He leans forward and runs his thumb along my bottom lip. "If I fucking feel like it, I'll do a lot of things with Master to our little doll."

"What kinds of things?" I roll onto my back, imploring him with my gaze.

"Painful things."

"I like it when you hurt me." I sit up, despite the sting on my ass, and lock my fingers behind his neck. Bringing him down to my mouth, I smile against his lips. "I like it when you take care of me too. You know best, Monster."

"Such a good doll," he croons. "Now, let's get you cleaned up and in one of your pretty dresses. I want you to look perfect for Master."

"I want to look perfect for you too," I tell him with a happy sigh.

He grins as he scoops me into his arms. "You look beyond perfect, Bethany. You *are* perfect."

I can't help but think how *not* perfect my sister is.

Only *I* can be exactly what Master and Monster need.

I'm a perfect little doll.

I've been practicing for a very long time.

CHAPTER TWENTY-FOUR

~ Fractured ~

Viktor

DILLON HAS BEEN KEEPING ME here on purpose instead of moving me into the prison system on remand. He's making sleep impossible and offering me slop for food, knowing it will never pass my lips. He deprives me of basic human needs, then brings me into his little four-walled cage for questioning, thinking that without sleep and food, I'll forget who I trust and scream for the ones I love.

Falling into his trap will never happen.

He will not defeat me.

"Is my lawyer here yet?" I smile, feeling anything but smug. Inside, I'm crumbling at the thought of Elizabeth being pumped with chemicals to cure her of her inner monsters. She doesn't need curing just because they don't feel safe with the beast living within her.

"What is your full name?" the mundane officer asks.

"Which one?" I taunt, and this new arrogant bastard glares over at me.

Dillon must be off with his family. They circle this routine of someone new coming in to try to break me.

They're all pathetic. It's almost laughable. If I weren't in dire need of a shower and some shuteye, I'd enjoy the game.

If Vlad is indeed here to eradicate the one person who weakens me, then I won't be in here for much longer anyway. Vlad will bring this place down brick by brick if he needs to. Thoughts of him hurting Benjamin make me want to scream from the top of my lungs and rip my heart from my chest so I won't have to suffer the agony of it. Everything we've endured to finally be at a place where we accept we need each other will have been for nothing. He is more a part of me than I am, and Elizabeth completes us. He holds my soul and she my heart. I refuse to live in this world without them. The battle lines are drawn, and if anything has happened to Benjamin, no one will survive the war I will bring down on this world.

"Answer the damn question," the officer snaps.

"I'm quite parched, actually," I deadpan. "Would you mind ever so much and bring me a drink?"

"Of course, sir, what will it be? How about a whiskey on the rocks?" he mocks.

I'm tempted to use his tie to strangle him when the door suddenly opens and Dillon stands there looking worn out and tired. That fuckhead needs a vacation.

"Leave us," he tells this moron.

"It's getting pitiful now, Detective." I yawn and roll my shoulders. "It's like you're not even trying anymore." My heart nearly beats through my chest when Dillon moves into the room, and behind him, my brother follows. I stand and jar from my cuffs being chained to a hoop on the table. "Moy brat," I breathe.

"Mladshiy brat, rad videt tebya," he rattles off in our mother tongue.

I sigh and smile at him. "It's good to see you too. Please tell me you bring good news with you."

His brow collapses over his features and he nods for Dillon to leave the room.

"I fucking hate you cunts," Dillon growls, and if I weren't concerned with my brother's pinched features, I'd laugh.

The door slams shut and the room is silent for a beat.

"What troubles you, Vlad?" I dare not ask him about Benjamin in case Kami was lying and didn't in fact mention my monster to him, only told him I needed him.

Wishful thinking is beneath you, my inner thoughts tease.

"I've come to take you home, brat."

My chest heaves. I've yearned to hear those words for too long.

"Father sent for me?" I pray.

He comes around the table and rests his hand on my shoulder. "Otets became very sick, moy brat."

"Sick how?"

He taps a hand over his heart. "Heart attack, sudden."

My legs weaken and I find myself falling into the chair.

"I need to see him," I choke out.

"Otet passed into the afterlife."

An empty chill rinses through my veins.

My father is dead.

Dead.

I will never get his pardon. He will never tell me it

was a mistake to banish me.

"It's time to come home, Viktor. I need you by my side. We have an empire to run."

I can't focus. The hunger and sleep deprivation, mixed with this sorrow and confusion, come crashing into me all at once.

"I'm getting you out of here," he says. "You have outgrown the roots you've planted."

The door reopens, and Vlad points down to my cuffs. In the next moment, they're being taken from me. Hands aid me to stand and my feet shuffle forward with someone guiding me. The lights burn my retinas and I just want to close my eyes, the open wound in my chest expanding with every step I take.

"Benjamin," I mumble, desperate for his council, his comfort, his strength.

"Do not speak his name, Viktor," Vlad whispers into my ear, and my soul flees. He *does* know of him. He would have slaughtered him surely, thinking him a threat.

I can't go there.

I can't think about it.

For three years, Benjamin has filled a deep void inside me. And only recently, did I help him realize how we fit together. Pieces of a complicated puzzle.

I refuse to think of him as eliminated from the game.

That fucker has as many lives as a cat.

At least that's the hope I hold onto.

I can't breathe. Every bone in my body aches. We step outside. Wind and rain suddenly attack my skin, and it scalds like acid. The fire once burning so strong within me is doused to ashes. My life was just something to be broken down to nothing. Taking everything from me and banishing me led me to Benjamin. My dreams, my family, my pride—all stolen from me—but I rebuilt and harnessed my monsters and he came into my life, making everything else fade. He made everything I'd suffered worth it. Nothing mattered and was insignificant because I found him. The heartache, the betrayal, the dark, dark, dark days just led me to his soul, ravished and in need of healing. I did heal him, and he healed me in return.

Without him, I am empty again.

My eyes close and I mentally will Vlad to drive this car he's ushered me into off the closest bridge. It will make everything easier. Because killing the only person I thought I could still rely on is going to be one of the hardest things I've ever done.

I'm sorry, big brother.

Benjamin's life will need retribution, and all that stained his life will pay in blood. Including Vlad.

"Wake, brat."

Vlad's voice startles me. My lids open, blinking away the intrusion of his flashlight shining in my fucking eyes.

"What are you doing?" I bark, my voice hoarse from sleep.

"Checking to make sure you're not still delirious."

"I'm fine."

He smiles softly. "You're quite remarkable, Viktor. The life you created here is impressive. The man you're so taken with is quite the myth, the whispered boogeyman. I did my research. Klara was a fool to think I didn't know whom you surrounded yourself with. I can sniff out when someone is important. Different from everyone else. His need is quite something, and the girl…"

My body stiffens, and I can't breathe. "The *doll*."

His smile reaches up to his eyes. It's such a rare sight, I just gaze in amazement. "Her madness is extraordinary. I want to bottle it and sell it." He beams, winking at me. "Come," he orders, getting out the car.

The door opens and some giant guy nods his head at me. Stepping from the car, I walk side-by-side with my brother for the first time in decades.

"With Otet's passing," he starts, "I became heir of his empire, and I need you by my side, moy brat. Your exile died with Otet." I don't ask where Vika fits in. Without Benjamin and Elizabeth, I don't fit in anywhere. "I haven't been witness to your life, but your story is whispered on the lips of many. You grew into so much more than I ever thought possible. I admire the man you've become, and I'm proud of you, brat," he tells me. I want to bask in his pride and praise, but I'm broken.

"Viktor," a delicate, lyrical voice chimes from the steps of the stunning home we're in front of. Elizabeth stands there in a pretty burgundy dress, her hair in pigtails and socks pulled high over her knees. Am I dreaming her?

Thud.

A shadow creeps over her form.

Thud.

My monster comes to rest by her side, his wild brown eyes desperately seeking mine. Alive.

Thud.

I stagger toward the steps, and emotion nearly

cripples me as I take them in my arms. They smell of soap and vanilla and mine. They smell of fucking mine, and it's beautiful. It's so fucking perfect, I can't take the feelings storming inside my chest.

"You're home," Monster growls, relief flickering in his gaze.

"Is *this* home?" I ask, looking up at the house.

"No," Elizabeth whispers. She takes my hand and intertwines our fingers. Then, she threads her fingers with his. I reach for him, and he doesn't pull away. His grip is tight on mine. Together, we stand in a circle, like three fucked-up kids playing Ring Around the Rosy. "This. Us. *We're* home," she finishes.

I close my eyes and grit my teeth. It's as though my heart is going to claw its way up my throat and throw itself at the two people beside me.

"I want you all," Vlad announces from the bottom of the stairs, interrupting our reunion.

"What?"

He smirks as he regards us. "Let me paint this clear for you, brat. Life is short, and I'm done living mine without you in it. If they are your family, then they are my family, and they come with you back to your homeland. You're done here. There is nothing here for you any longer."

I turn to look at Elizabeth and Benjamin.

Benjamin gives me a hard stare, his eyes flickering with a thousand emotions, and nods. "I'm ready for a change of fucking scenery."

"Away from the people who want to separate us," our doll adds cheerily. "It's perfect. I've always wanted to travel."

"Then we will go," I agree, my tone soft despite the excitement bubbling up inside me.

"Great," Vlad says as he clasps a hand on my shoulder. "You don't know how happy this makes me, Viktor. Now, go and get some rest. My plane will be fueled and ready to leave by tomorrow."

I spent my entire life building The Vault and my reputation here, but it means nothing. In the end, it's all so goddamn irrelevant.

"Come inside, Viktor," Benjamin grunts. "I have something to show you."

I follow them both into the house, relief so strong coursing through my body, I feel like I've popped a hundred Xanax. Benjamin leads us through a lobby entranceway and up a swirling staircase. Old paintings in thick gold frames adorn the walls and old patterned carpet line the stairs. It reminds me of our childhood home. Benjamin keeps peering over his shoulder at me, and it makes my heart pound like a rabid beast inside its confines. His walking is much better on that ankle and he doesn't appear to be in pain from his injuries. Elizabeth dances up the stairs next to me, invading my space and filling it with her whimsical character. She keeps reaching for my hand, our little doll vying for my attention, but Benjamin seems to like to torment her. He swats her away and grips my elbow in a possessive way. Strong. Powerful. Unwavering.

"She's quite the naughty doll," he groans over his shoulder before stopping at a door.

Pushing inside, he gestures me in behind him. Elizabeth is on my heels and heat begins to simmer under my flesh. A huge four-poster bed dominates the room, and

I feel like I've added a cocaine kicker to those endorphins soaking through my veins. My chest is already panting at just the idea of what will transpire in this room. Benjamin wastes no time grabbing his dolly from behind, wrapping his arm around her shoulder and cupping her chin in his hand.

"Our dolly has been a very bad girl," he snarls, stealing a kiss from her open mouth, her lipstick smudging. Benjamin's eyes flare wide and seem to liquefy when he sees the mess he's created. "You've ruined your lips, Doll."

She brings her finger to her mouth and bites down on it in an innocent way that has my dick standing at attention and raging to be released from the confines of my slacks.

Benjamin must feel the same because he tears at her dress, shredding the material and baring her naked flesh beneath. He tugs and pulls until she stands there in nothing but white lacy panties and her socks. Strips of material scatter the floor at her feet. "You ruined my dress," she pouts, and he smirks.

"You will have to make a new one. A better one. Now, take those panties off and show Master what a bad girl you were earlier."

Her eyes sparkle as she looks at me when he says Master. It's euphoric to see her stare at me with such intensity. She hooks her fingers into her panties and glides them down the silky-smooth skin of her thighs, letting them drop to her ankles and stepping out of them.

"Now, turn around and bend over," Benjamin instructs.

Her bare pussy is smooth and inviting, but it's soon

stolen from view as she turns to bare her ass to us. Red hand prints mar her perfect apple bottom. Benjamin splays a palm over one cheek and beckons for me to come closer with a crook of his other finger.

"She was a bad dolly and needed punishment."

Licking my lips, I admire his work before flashing him a wolfish smile. "You went easy on her I see."

He gives me a sinister glare, his lips twitching as though he's fighting a grin. "Smell her." He parts her ass cheeks and her puckered hole is slightly red and battered.

"You took her ass," I observe, and almost come in my pants at the mental image.

"Why don't you taste and find out?" he urges.

Yes. Yes. Yes.

Dropping to my knees, I grip her thighs in my hands. He moves to stand in front of her and peers down at me over her back.

"Taste *us*," he orders, unzipping his slacks and ripping off his shirt. Within a second, he's naked and gripping our doll's head. He shoves his cock straight down her throat, and she gags and moans at the same time.

She likes it rough.

He hammers his hips forward, fucking her face with vigor. She slurps and groans in pleasure around his thick length, and I can't just watch anymore. Flicking my tongue against her tight asshole, I taste a salty tang from my monster's cum being there hours before. It's such a distinctive flavor on my tongue that has me groaning. I swipe up and down her ass, coating her in saliva, and breach her hole with my finger, moving my tongue lower to her perfect throbbing pussy. She's dripping wet and she tastes sweet and sour.

It's fucking heavenly.

My dick throbs in my slacks, desperate for some relief. Using my free hand, I push my slacks down over my hips and past my thighs to my knees. My dick springs free and slaps against my stomach. Taking the heavy weight in my hand, I stroke myself as I fuck her holes with my fingers and tongue. The dewy pre-cum seeping from my bulging head aids my effort. She's suddenly pulled away from me, and I mourn the loss.

"Take off your shirt." Benjamin orders.

And I don't argue. I rip the material from my body, sending buttons flying in all directions. Benjamin picks Elizabeth up and tosses her on the bed like she's a real doll—his plaything.

"Spread your legs, doll," he barks out.

She's giddy and compliant, spreading herself across the bed, her legs reaching the entire width and resting on the two poles jutting up from the frame.

"Climb on our dolly, Master, and fuck her until she's passes the hell out," he instructs.

Her innocent eyes find mine, and she pleads, "Oh, please fuck me, Master. Fuck me hard."

This heady sensation is consuming. I've never felt this turned on in all my life. I've always felt out of place, never finding the right balance of pleasure until now.

"Are you sure?" I ask Monster. I'm still unsure about where his thoughts are in all of this.

He snarls in irritation. "Fuck her while I fuck you. Know who *owns* you."

Our eyes meet for a moment. Fury and madness

blaze in his gaze. And heat. Desire and need. Everything that makes him who he is swirls around just below the surface, waiting to be devoured by me.

I climb onto the edge of the bed and mount the tiny doll beneath me. Her tits peak like little hilltops and her hard nipples scream ruby-red, begging to be simulated. I suck one into my mouth and roll my tongue over the nub. She wriggles beneath me, causing my dick to slap against her pussy lips.

"Please fuck me," she whines, and it's music to my ears.

Benjamin fists my hair and growls. "Line yourself up, now."

I part her pussy and prod at her tight hole. Benjamin spits on my ass and spreads my cheeks, rubbing his saliva down to the tight, puckered entry. Shoving my head forward, he stabs at me a few times, then finds home, slamming into me. My hips jut forward, and I bury myself to the hilt inside our doll. We scream in unison—pain, pleasure, exhilaration, all overwhelming us. We become an in-sync movement, gliding in and out of each other with perfect precision. Pleasure warms and spreads throughout my body, coating me in a sheen of sweat that aids our movements. Skin slapping against skin, grunt and groans become our soundtrack. Benjamin is without mercy as he pounds his cock into me, forcing me to fuck the life out of Elizabeth. Her body is sucking onto me like a goddamn vampire, her walls squeezing and contracting. She's ravenous as she screams and claws at my back, opening the flesh.

Benjamin pulls out of me and slaps me hard across

the ass cheek. "Move her on top." His breath is coming out in ragged pants. I love when he loses control.

Obeying him, I flip onto my back, and she rocks her hips over me, her tits bouncing with every enthusiastic twirl. Benjamin crawls up behind her and wraps something around her neck. It's a tie, one of mine from my house. He grins down at me, and she moans as she writhes over me.

I'm going to fucking come.

Jesus Christ this is hot.

I grab her hips to slow her wriggling, but she fights my grip even when I tighten to cause pain. Her eyes ignite the harder I try to restrain her movement. Benny pushes her down over me and keeps hold of the ends of the tie like they're reigns. He spits into his other palm and Elizabeth's mouth drops open. She moans and gargles as he enters her ass.

Fuck.

Fuck.

Fuck.

I can feel him inside her, his cock pushing past the rings of muscle and caressing me from inside her. My balls tighten and heat spreads up my spine. I can't hold off much longer.

Fuck.

Monster powers into her, causing her body to jar forward over and over against the restraints of the necktie. Her eyes are watering and she's gasping for breath. Her pussy clamps around me and her entire body spasms with her orgasm.

Monster follows her over, and I feel the heat of him

empty into her as I roar out my own release. Elizabeth drops against my chest, her body twitching and limp.

"She passed out," I say with a laugh, and Benjamin stands there, sweat glistening over his tattooed torso, the bloody words Jessica carved into him risen and red with wet blood. We angered them.

His fiery gaze remains on me. All the words he wants to speak conveyed only in his eyes. I gently move Elizabeth to the space next to me, then reach up and pull Benjamin into my arms. His muscular frame falls against mine, and I bring his head to my chest and curl my arms around his impressive physique.

With Benjamin, you must tread lightly.

But right now, I just want to keep him close.

"I thought I lost you," I confess into the room, my voice but a whisper.

"I'm right fucking here and I'm not going anywhere," he confirms.

My eyes close, and I'm content for the first time in my entire life.

"Is going back to Russia what you want?" he suddenly asks.

"I think it's a sensible option and my brother is an ally."

"And what about your sister?"

Vika.

I sigh heavily. "We can cross that bridge if and when we come to it."

"I'll throw her off it," he grunts.

With a grin on my lips, I relax and let sleep steal me away.

CHAPTER TWENTY-FIVE

~ *Shattered* ~

Dillon

Jade is staring at me openmouthed at my suggestion. "You want us to just pack up and move—start a whole new life?"

"It's not that crazy," I tell her with a sigh. "I'm fucking tired, baby. Tired of losing to the bad guy and tired of waiting for Benny to finally decide to kill you."

"You said he's gone to Russia," she snaps.

"Yeah, but who fucking knows if he will decide to come back. I can't risk it anymore. I can't do this shit for much longer."

She sits and then stands. Sits and then stands. "What about our jobs?"

"Quit."

"Just like that?" she screeches.

"Yes. People do it all the time. I want us to start our own business. Private investigation. Work the hours we decide and take the cases we fucking want to take. Help people who need us."

She folds her arms. "You've really thought hard about this?"

"Yes."

"And your mom and Jasmine?"

"They have nothing keeping them here."

"What about Elise and Marcus?"

"He's on board."

Her eyes nearly pop from her skull. "You've spoken to him about this?"

"We've spoke about it in the past. He's sick of the job too, and at some point, you just need to know when to throw in the towel before it scars you too deep." I can't help but tease. "Josey's not coming. You can breathe easy. She thinks she's going to become a badass detective."

I don't want her to fight me on this. I just want her to *not* be my feisty-ass fighter for once and know when to see I'm done with this shit. I need her to be on board.

I want the easy life. The country. For my kids to be safe and me not to have an aneurism every time they want to play outside, or fuck, even go to school.

"So, we take everyone with us?"

"Yes."

"Okay."

Wait. What?

"Babe?" I say, cautious I misheard her.

"No, you're right. Dammit, you're right. Let's move somewhere quiet and build a big old farmhouse and get four dogs, a horse, and geese." She beams, and it's been so long since I've seen her look so carefree and excited. "Josey can come visit whenever she wants."

I scoop her up and kiss her lips over and over. "And we can make five new babies," I growl against her mouth, and she slaps my shoulders.

"No. No more babies. Just Animals. Let Elise do the breeding." She giggles, and I want to stop time and live in the moment of her laugh.

"I feel like some negotiations are in order," I tease.

"Nope," she says with a smile. "I'm done."

"Bet I can change your mind once the doctor clears you to have sex," I brag as I set her to her feet and let her feel how hard she makes me.

Her eyes widen and she lifts her chin. "You'll have to do a *lot* of convincing."

"I'll convince you *all night* every night."

"Honestly, Dillon, you're relentless."

"I hug too!" a cheerful little voice screeches as small footsteps thunder our way.

We both laugh when MJ hugs our legs.

"Let's go get our happy ending," I tell my wife before dropping a kiss to her forehead. I run my fingers through our daughter's hair.

Jade sighs, but there's a smile in her voice. "It's about damn time."

"It's about damn time," MJ mimics, flashing us a toothy grin.

EPILOGUE

~ *Broken* ~

Benny
Russia
Several months later…

I SIT IN THE LEATHER armchair across from Viktor's desk and watch him while he works. He's always in his element when he's running shit and controlling other people's lives. And Vlad wasn't joking. The moment we set foot in his homeland, the fucker put him to work. Viktor tells me this year's The V Games—I'm still not sure what the fuck they are—will be the best yet. That our doll and I will love this shit. I'm looking forward to it.

His brows are furrowed as he taps away on the computer. I can tell he's stressed. He feels the need to do a good job for his brother. Viktor gets up early in the morning and ends up obsessing over his work until late in the evenings when we force him to bed.

But he's happy.

He promised we'd be happy, the three of us, and he was right.

"What's our little doll up to today?" he questions, his thoughts mirroring mine.

I smirk. "The usual."

At this, a wolfish grin spreads over his face. His amber eyes flicker with wickedness as he rolls away from his desk in his high-back leather desk chair and threads his fingers together. Fucker looks like some evil villain about to tell me how he's going to take over the world.

"She's a naughty little thing." His gaze roves over my chest before settling on my mouth for a brief moment. "And what are you up to today?"

I stand and shove my hands into my jean pockets. "Keeping tabs on everyone. Working on *the house*. The usual."

He rises from his chair and smooths out the wrinkles from the front of his charcoal-grey slacks. His fitted white dress shirt is tucked in to his pants and an expensive-ass snakeskin belt his brother gave him hugs his narrow waist. Unusual for Viktor, he's not wearing his jacket or tie. The top couple buttons are undone and his sleeves are rolled up to just below the elbow, revealing his veiny forearms.

His forearms get my dick hard.

Just last night, those veins in question bulged as he gripped our little dolly's throat while he fucked her raw.

Yep, those forearms get me painfully hard.

"Any new additions I should approve, Mr. Handyman?" His brow quirks up.

I laugh and shrug. "I know your tastes by now."

He walks over to the window overlooking the expanse of his property—of our property—and folds his arms over his chest. I flank him and peer down at the scene below.

Our doll hardly stands out among the snow-covered earth in her furry white coat. The hood hides her even more, but it's her dark hair that escapes and blows in the wind that gives her away. As if she feels our eyes on her, she turns and grins up at us. Viktor waves at her, and I nod my head. She turns away and continues walking, disappearing under some trees.

"Is she going to town?"

"She's having a craving."

"It's too bad," Viktor mutters.

"Why's that?" My dick throbs in my pants.

He turns and steps into my space, his heat scorching me through my thin, long-sleeved T-shirt. "I would have given her a treat."

I grip his throat and lean my forehead against his. He smells of vodka. I swear, they all drink that shit over here. Lucky for him, I like the way it tastes on his tongue. As if on cue, he parts his mouth and accepts my ravenous kiss. With Viktor, sometimes I want to suck his soul right from his body. I want what makes him...*him*. It hides below his surface, and I crave to cut right into him to pull it out so I can devour it.

I groan when he rubs his palm against my cock through my jeans.

"One of these days," he growls against my mouth, "I'm going to bend *you* over my desk and let *you* feel *me* inside you."

Fire ripples through me.

Furious and malevolent.

When he taunts my beast, I want to destroy him. Sometimes, I think he does it on purpose. I've let him blow me more times than I can count now. And sometimes, the sneaky bastard gets freaky on me. I've come several times so hard, I was nearly blinded when he did some weird shit to my balls and even pushed his finger up my ass a time or two.

"You can't take me," I snap as I squeeze his throat.

His amber eyes seem to glow with evil. "Oh, Benjamin, but I can. I just always *let* you win our little games."

I narrow my gaze at him. "Fucking liar."

"Don't get mad when I eventually tame my monster and ride him all the way into hell," he murmurs, his teeth nipping at my jaw, then ear. "Even monsters need to be subdued every now and again."

His hands work to unfasten my jeans and he manages to push them down my thighs. The moment he grips my cock, I groan, my hand loosening around his throat.

My eyes close as he strokes me. Heat pools in my belly as desperation to ram my dick so far up his ass he screams overwhelms me. But while I'm fantasizing, the fucker strikes.

With lightning fast reflexes, he twists me and shoves me forward. My hands fall forward and I catch myself against the mahogany surface of his desk instead of face planting. A rage-filled roar escapes me, but then something tightens around my throat. That asshole has his goddamn belt around my neck.

I jerk and jolt, but he's ruthless as he pins me against the desk. He yanks on the belt, and I hiss for breath. My gut instinct is to claw at the belt, but it's digging too far into my flesh to do anything about it.

"That's it, Monster. Lie down for your master." His voice is manic and violent. My cock lurches with need. "Good boy."

He presses his length against the crack of my ass, and I freeze. Panic and terror rise in my throat, but remain trapped where the belt has me captive. I don't know why I'm freaking the fuck out, but all I can think about is how I'll cut open his belly and yank his intestines out the moment he releases me.

"Relax," he says in the authoritative tone he wields like a sword. "I'll make it feel good."

He spits from behind me, and I know it's coming. Closing my eyes, I wait for the pain. The tip of his cock is wet as it slides along my crack. He pushes it against the hole he's only ever breached with his fingers. That fuck knew what he was doing this whole time. He was getting me ready.

Viktor.

Always planning ten moves ahead.

Always a fucking game with him.

My thoughts blank away as white-hot pain sears through me. His fucking cock is an anaconda and it's sliding inside me painfully slow. I claw at his desk, sending shit careening to the floor. It doesn't deter him as he sinks deeper inside me. I start to black out from lack of air when he finally releases the belt. I rip it away from my throat, desperate for oxygen.

"Who do you belong to?" he taunts as he slowly fucks me from behind.

"I'll fucking destroy you," I seethe.

He laughs, like a fucking maniac. "Then I better make this good for the both of us since my time is limited." He rakes his fingers down my back, and my nerves come alive. My ass clenches and I shudder as a foreign sensation of pleasure spikes up my spine. He leans forward and his mouth presses kisses on my shoulder blade. Worshipping. Loving. Needy. As he fucks me like I'm something prized and revered, I finally get it.

I own him no matter what.

Whether I'm down here, on top, or with my dick down his throat, I own them both. They're mine. My perfect little dolls.

"Yes," he groans, as if he can hear my thoughts. He slides his arm beneath me and lifts. I rest on my fists, now away from the desk. Our skin makes a slapping sound as he drives into me. When his hand wraps around my cock that seeps with pre-cum, I hiss in pleasure. "Mine."

Maybe the motherfucker isn't crazy.

This shit feels really fucking good.

I groan and grunt as he masterfully plays my body. For once, I relinquish control and let him do as he fucking pleases. He's an expert, and soon, my orgasm, starting deep inside me, crashes through me. It's intense and wicked as hell. I nearly collapse, but he's got a death grip on me. He groans, and his heat surges inside me. It sets me off, and I explode with a sharp gasp. My cum splatters all over his desk and paperwork.

I'm shaking from all the sensations surging through me, but the moment I see a memo from Vlad soaked with my cum, I start laughing.

"You messed up my desk, you asshole," he grumbles, amusement in his voice.

He eases out of me and steps away. I jerk my pants up quickly before turning to attack him. But the moment our eyes meet, I halt. His dark, always styled hair, has fallen over his sweaty brow and his amber eyes are on fire. His dark pink lips are parted as he pants, and his dripping cock hangs at half-mast just above where his slacks are pulled halfway down his thighs.

"You're fucking filthy," I growl, waving my hand at his disheveled appearance.

His lips quirk up on one side as he pulls his slacks up and tucks his dick away. "I've been called worse."

My fury and rage have simmered.

He's my best friend.

My motherfucking brother.

The devil has my soul in his steely grip.

"Let's go find our doll, Monster."

And we do.

"It's not fair," Doll pouts, her bright pink lips pursed together.

I lift a brow. "Life's not fair."

She rolls her eyes and gives me a shove. "You suck."

Viktor snags her by the wrist and yanks her to him, planting a wet kiss on her plump lips. "Actually, you're the only one who sucks around here."

"I hate when you punks gang up on me," she grumbles, but light dances in her eyes.

I stalk over to her and rub my palm over the swell of her stomach. Inside her, she carries life. Whether it's mine or Viktor's, I don't care. It's ours. A fucking baby.

"Did you satisfy your craving, Doll?" I ask before pressing a kiss to her nose.

She beams at me. Innocent. Sweet. Playful. Perfect.

"I did."

"And tell me about it," I urge. I love hearing all about her cravings. It fucking sings to my black heart.

She pulls away and takes each of our hands. "Let me show you."

We let her wind us through the massive estate until we reach the underbelly of the home. *The house* as we call it. *The doll house.* Viktor unlocks the door and flips the switch that illuminates the stairs.

Screams.

Like music in a symphony only the three of us can create.

"Has Viktor seen the newest addition to *the house*?" she asks me.

"Not yet."

"Oh, goodie!" she chirps as she releases our hands.

We follow her down the steps. The pink dress she wears is hand sewn. I helped her with this one, because we had to allow room in the front for her stomach, but the design is all her. It's short and reveals her lacy panties with each step she takes. My dick is already alive and eager for more play time. Always play time with these two.

She reaches the bottom of the steps and turns on another light that seems to incite more screaming. We follow behind her, amused, as she flits about *the house*. She looks in each window and admires the rooms I painstakingly decorated to her specifications. Inside each space holds a pretty little doll. Pretty little dolls our perfect doll has selected. Dolls she's befriended and invited to her home. Dolls she's decided to keep forever.

Such a spoiled little girl.

"Please," the doll named Luna sobs as she bangs her fists against the Plexiglass. "Let me out of here!" The doll's face is now disfigured. She's been carved with jagged lines all over her flesh, as if she's been dropped and cracked in a hundred different ways.

Viktor walks over to her, his lip curling up as he inspects the room she's in. She's taken to smearing her shit all over the place. Did she really think we'd let her out if she was a filthy little doll? Bitch can sit and suffer the stink. That's punishment enough.

"Come," our doll chirps.

We pass the other many, many crying dolls until we reach the end. The newest "addition." The room is all pink, and I painted hearts on the walls earlier this afternoon. It's perfect. All we need is a doll to fill it.

"This one. I've named her Dolly Elise," she tells us, a wicked grin on her lips. She rubs her belly as she peers in. "Of course, it isn't the *real* Elise, but close enough."

Viktor and I come to stand behind her. The girl inside is about our doll's age and huddled in the corner. Her eyeliner is over the top and her clothes are indeed expensive, looking every bit the part of snotty bitch like our doll's twin. As soon as she sees us, she jolts to her feet and starts crying. Her lips frantically move as Russian spits from her lips.

Viktor laughs.

"Her daddy will give us anything we ask for," he translates. "Anything. Cars. Money. Property. Whatever we want is ours. Just let her go."

Our doll huffs. "Fuck that. I don't want that stuff. I want a Dolly Elise."

The girl inside the cell glares at our doll, yelling more Russian at her.

"Oh, no," Viktor chides. "You aren't allowed to talk to our perfect doll like that. That'll get you punished."

Our perfect doll claps her hands together gleefully. "Let me!"

I pull her against me and kiss the top of her head as I splay my palms over her belly. "Not so fast. You're in no shape to punish anyone."

Viktor begins unbuttoning his shirt. "I'll make sure she knows what a bad doll she is," he tells us, his amber eyes flaming with evil. He sheds his shirt and holds out his palm.

Our doll grumbles, but produces a knife she'd hidden in her garter belt under her dress. "Make her look like all the rest."

Viktor leans in and kisses her mouth. "Of course. You know you always get what you want." His eyes flicker to mine. "Sometimes I wonder who the *real* master around here is." I smirk. The fucker is right as hell. This doll of ours pulls the goddamn strings, and fuck if I don't enjoy every twisted second of it.

His fingers fly over the keypad and his entry is granted.

Our doll bounces on her toes, her excitement palpable. I squeeze her tight as we enjoy the show. Viktor prowls inside, stalking his prey. The muscles in his back flex and tighten, his tattoos seemingly alive as he moves toward her. She screams and throws stuff at him, decorations I worked so hard to install, but he's not deterred. With graceful, fluid motions, he begins his masterpiece.

Blood sprays across the pink wall.

Our doll screams with joy.

Dolly Elise screams for other reasons.

Slash. Slash. Slash.

Viktor pins the rich dolly to the floor with his knee in her stomach and artfully decorates her face. Every so often, his manic eyes seek us out. He finds us. His family. He smiles. And we smile back.

When he finishes and the girl has long passed out from pain, he stands. Blood coats his front and face. His forearms I fucking love so much drip with crimson. He strides back through the doorway and our doll closes it until it latches and locks.

The three of us peer inside and stare at the newest addition.

One more.

Our pretty broken dolls.

"We're going to need a bigger house," our perfect doll murmurs. "What now?"

I chuckle as I unzip the back of her dress. It falls and pools at her feet, leaving her in nothing but her lacy panties and knee-highs. I rub my palm along her ass and growl into her ear.

"Run, run, run, little doll. Monster and Master are ready to play."

The End

Join us for the spinoff…

The V Games Series—Coming soon!

PLAYLIST
Listen on Spotify

"Monster" by Meg & Dia
"Dark Side" by Bishop Briggs
"Heathens" by Twenty One Pilots
"Desire" by Meg Myers
"Sucker For Pain" by Lil Wayne
"Bullet With Butterfly Wings" by The Smashing Pumpkins
"Monster" by Meg Myers
"Game of Survival" by Ruelle
"Monsters" by Ruelle
"Psycho" by Muse
"Tainted Love" by Marilyn Manson
"Run, Run, Run" by Tokio Hotel
"We're In This Together" by Nine Inch Nails
"Take Out the Gunman" by Chevelle
"Stand by Me" by Ki:Theory
"Are You Alone Now?" by Dead Sea Empire
"Obsession" by Golden State
"The Monster" by Eminem
"Doll Parts" by Hole
"Psycho Killer" by Talking Heads
"Everybody Wants to Rule the World" by Lorde
"Psychotic Girl" by The Black Keys

ACKNOWLEDGMENTS FROM Ker Dukey

I would like to thank you, the reader, for coming on this journey with us. Kristi and I built a world of chaos and depravity, and you embraced it and became our little dollies. Your love and support made writing this series, and these incredibly complex characters, a pleasure.

Kristi, thanks for creating magic with me (raises a glass). Here is to many more moments of magic.

A special mention to all the wonderful blogs who shared everything Dolls. Without you, we couldn't share our worlds.

Monica Black, our editor, thank you for always being enthusiastic, and being there to hit the ground running when we drop the MS on you. Stacey Blake, you make all our books so pretty, you're amazing, and we wouldn't want anyone else to touch our baby.

A big THANK YOU to Nicole from INDIESAGEPR for reveals and release blitz.

Thank you to K's Proofreaders, you have an eagle eye, and it's appreciated that you take the time to catch any snags for us.

Terrie my PA, thanks for handling my hecticness ← thats not a word but it sums up what you have to put up with.

Thank you to Nicky and Rosa for keeping my group running and all the DarKER stalKER's for always wanting more.

ACKNOWLEDGEMENTS FROM
K. Webster

A huge thank you to Ker Dukey riding out this series with me. I've had a blast and hope to write plenty more projects together in the future!

Thank you to my husband, Matt. You're always there to love and support me. I can't thank you enough. I'll always be your favorite doll.

I want to send out a GIANT thanks to all the supportive dollies out there. Your morbid curiosity, thirst for more, or general love for villains is what has made this series such a success. Benny loves *all* his little dolls. Continue to be good little dolls and we might give you more of your beloved Benjamin. Love you guys for being so awesome and excited about our characters! (Fun fact: The title headers in *Pretty Broken Dolls* are synonyms of the word "broken.")

A huge thanks to Elizabeth Clinton and Ella Stewart and Misty Walker. Thank you always being so supportive and quick to read my stuff no matter what. You are great friends!

Thank you to Liana Vanoyan for checking our Russian! You rock, girl!

I want to thank the people who either beta read this book or proofed it early. You all gave me great feedback and the support I needed to carry on. You all give me helpful ideas to make my stories better and give me incredible encouragement. I appreciate all of your comments and suggestions.

A big thank you to my author friends who have given me your friendship and your support. You have no idea how much that means to me.

Thank you to all of my blogger friends both big and small that go above and beyond to always share my stuff. You all rock! #AllBlogsMatter

I'm especially thankful for my Krazy for K Webster's Books reader group. You ladies are wonderful with your support and friendship. Each and every single one of you is amazingly supportive and caring. I love that we can all be weird page sniffers together.

A huge thanks to Monica with Word Nerd Editing for taking care of another one of our precious dolly books and making it as perfect as it could be!

Thank you Stacey Blake for making this book GORGEOUS like always! Love you!

A big thanks to my PR gal, Nicole Blanchard. You are fabulous at what you do and keep me on track! Also a big thanks to the ladies over at The Hype PR!

Lastly but certainly not least of all, thank you to all of the wonderful readers out there that are willing to hear my stories and enjoy my characters like I do. It means the world to me!

ABOUT THE AUTHOR
Ker Dukey

My books all tend to be darker romance, edge of you seat, angst filled reads. My advice to my readers when starting one of my titles…prepare for the unexpected.

I have always had a passion for storytelling, whether it be through lyrics or bed time stories with my sisters growing up.

My mum would always have a book in her hand when I was young and passed on her love for reading, inspiring me to venture into writing my own. I tend to have a darker edge to my writing. Not all love stories are made from light; some are created in darkness but are just as powerful and worth telling.

When I'm not lost in the world of characters I love spending time with my family. I'm a mum and that comes first in my life but when I do get down time I love attending music concerts or reading events with my younger sister.

News Letter sign up
www.Authorkerdukey.com
www.facebook.com/KerDukeyauthor

Contact me here
Ker: Kerryduke34@gmail.com
Ker's PA : terriesin@gmail.com

ABOUT THE AUTHOR

K Webster

K Webster is the author of dozens of romance books in many different genres including taboo romance, dark romance, contemporary romance, historical romance, paranormal romance, romantic suspense, and erotic romance. When not spending time with her husband of many, many years and two adorable children, she's active on social media connecting with her readers.

Her other passions besides writing include reading and graphic design. K can always be found in front of her computer chasing her next idea and taking action. She looks forward to the day when she will see one of her titles on the big screen.

Join K Webster's newsletter to receive a couple of updates a month on new releases and exclusive content. To join, all you need to do is go here http://authorkwebster.us10.list-manage.com/subscribe?u=36473e274a1bf9597b508ea72&id=96366bb08e).

Facebook: www.facebook.com/authorkwebster
Blog: authorkwebster.wordpress.com/
Twitter:twitter.com/KristiWebster
Email: kristi@authorkwebster.com
Goodreads:
www.goodreads.com/user/show/10439773-k-webster
Instagram: instagram.com/kristiwebster

KER'S BOOKS

Titles by Ker include:

Empathy series
Empathy
Desolate
Vacant
Deadly

The Deception series
FaCade
Cadence
Beneath Innocence - Novella

The Broken Series
The Broken
The Broken Parts Of Us
The Broken Tethers That Bind Us – Novella
The Broken Forever - Novella

The Men By Numbers Series
Ten
Six

Drawn to you series
Drawn to you
Lines Drawn

Standalone novels:
My soul Keeper
Lost
I see you
The Beats In Rift
Devil

The Pretty Little dolls series:
Pretty Stolen Dolls
Pretty Lost Dolls
Pretty New Doll

Titles coming soon:
Lost Boy

K'S BOOKS

The Breaking the Rules Series:
Broken
Wrong
Scarred
Mistake
Crushed

The Vegas Aces Series:
Rock Country
Rock Heart
Rock Bottom

The Becoming Her Series:
Becoming Lady Thomas
Becoming Countess Dumont
Becoming Mrs. Benedict

2 Lovers Series:
Text 2 Lovers
Hate 2 Lovers
Thieves 2 Lovers

Pretty Little Dolls Series:
Pretty Stolen Dolls
Pretty Lost Dolls
Pretty New Doll
Pretty Broken Dolls

Taboo Treats:
Bad Bad Bad
Easton
Crybaby

Alpha & Omega Duet:
Alpha & Omega
Omega & Love

War & Peace Series:
This is War, Baby
This is Love, Baby
This Isn't Over, Baby
This Isn't You, Baby
This is Me, Baby
This Isn't Fair, Baby
This is the End, Baby

Standalone Novels:
Apartment 2B
Love and Law
Moth to a Flame
Erased
The Road Back to Us
Surviving Harley
Give Me Yesterday
Running Free
Dirty Ugly Toy
Zeke's Eden
Sweet Jayne
Untimely You
Mad Sea
Whispers and the Roars
Schooled by a Senior
B-Sides and Rarities
Notice
Blue Hill Blood by Elizabeth Gray
The Wild

Made in the USA
Columbia, SC
27 October 2017